My Name Is America

The Journal of William Thomas Emerson

✢

A Revolutionary War Patriot

BY BARRY DENENBERG

Scholastic Inc. New York

Boston, Massachusetts
Summer 1774

The Lord's Mysterious Ways

My name is Will.

William Thomas Emerson is my full name, in honor of my papa, only he's dead now. So is everyone else.

We used to have a farm in Menotomy, a village not far from Boston. My sister, Mama, and Papa and me had just sat down to supper when it happened. The storm had been brewing all day. The thunder was rolling in and rattling the roof and the lightning crackled so loud and hard I thought the sky would shatter into a thousand pieces and come down all over the house.

They were gone—all of them—just like that. People say I was lucky because I was just stunned when the lightning hit and because I didn't open my eyes until the next morning.

They say all the plates just melted right on to the table. I can't tell you if that's true because I don't remember much.

I was ten. My birthday was just the week before. Mr. Heath took me for a while till they decided what to do with me now that I had no family. Mr. Heath said that the ways of the Lord

5

are mysterious and that I should never fear throwing myself on His mercy, which didn't make any sense to me then and doesn't make much sense to me now. Then he told me I would be bound out to the Marshes. They would take care of me and see to it that I was brought up right and in return I would help Mr. Marsh with the farm work.

They didn't have any children of their own, the Marshes, that's why they decided to take me in. At least that's what Mr. Heath told me. What Mr. Heath didn't tell me was that Mr. Marsh was a drinking man or that he would beat me till I was black and blue. I guess he didn't tell me that, Mr. Heath, because he was so busy telling me about the Lord's mysterious ways.

And Mrs. Marsh wasn't much of a help. She spent most of her day looking to see if Mr. Marsh was coming and, once he was home, shaking like a leaf. It was not a happy circumstance.

I took it for as long as I could. Two years. Then I couldn't take it anymore and ran away.

I waited till I could hear Mr. Marsh's heavy breathing. That meant he was asleep and nothing could wake him. Nothing. I could have marched out of there with a band playing and he wouldn't have stirred. I took my knife with me just in case. The one Papa gave me for my birthday.

Mr. Wilson's Proposal

I walked the trodden path till daybreak, heading, I hoped, for Boston. I must have fallen asleep because the next thing I knew I was being shaken by a serious-looking fellow who was puffing furiously at a red clay pipe that he held tightly clenched in his teeth. He said his name was Wilson. His voice was strong and sharp—it made you take notice. He said he wanted to know why I was sleeping by the side of the road and not home where I belonged. His face was covered with a light coating of dust from the road and for a time I thought maybe I was dreaming.

I told him I didn't have a home and was going to Boston to find work. He seemed to be giving this a great deal of thought. Finally, he spoke, saying, "That is a miraculous coincidence." I wasn't sure what he meant by that, but fortunately he explained—he, too, was on his way to Boston and would be pleased to have me accompany him in his one-horse carriage and, if I were willing, hear a proposal he had.

During the journey Mr. Wilson asked me why I didn't have a home. I told him what had happened to me up till then, talking as fast as I could because Mr. Wilson kept saying, "Get to the point, get to the point."

Just as we were about to enter through the town gates we were stopped by two British soldiers who looked inside the carriage and wanted to know who we were and where we came from. Mr. Wilson answered them politely, although the soldiers were rude.

The Seven Stars Tavern

It was thanks to him that I met Mrs. Thompson, who owns the Seven Stars Tavern, which is where I am now. It's located on the corner of King Street and Pudding Lane.

Mr. Wilson is one of Mrs. Thompson's boarders. Well, actually, right now he's her only boarder. His room is the only one on the top floor and the devil help you if you go in without knocking. Mr. Wilson doesn't like to be disturbed, especially when he's working on one of his pamphlets or writing an article for the newspaper.

During the trip to Boston all Mr. Wilson told me was that he was sure Mrs. Thompson could use help from a strong boy like me. I'm small for my age, but I am strong. Mr. Wilson was right. Mrs. Thompson could use the help. I could tell that just by looking around. The place was a mess. Chairs turned over this way and that, half-filled glasses and plates of food just sitting there with flies buzzing all around.

It was very late when we arrived and there was no one in the tavern. Mr. Wilson told me to have a seat and not go running off anywhere. He crouched down real low when he said that so he could look directly at me. I was sure his pale blue eyes were going to bore a hole right through my head. Mr. Wilson gives you the feeling he isn't someone you want to cross. And besides, where was I going to go?

He was gone for a long time so I rested some. When he returned he had Mrs. Thompson with him. She had a kind face, I could see that right off, and she looked tired to the bone. Mr. Wilson said he had explained everything that had happened to me from the night of the storm till now.

Mr. Wilson said I could stay here if I wanted—there was a small room in the cellar and I could sleep there. In return, he said, I would have to help Mrs. Thompson and do all that was asked of me.

I took a quick look at Mrs. Thompson while he was talking. She was listening politely and not showing much of what she was thinking, just wiping her hands on her apron. I said that was agreeable to me and then Mrs. Thompson showed me the room in the cellar.

If it wasn't for Mr. Wilson and Mrs. Thompson I don't know what would have become of me. Someday I hope to repay them for their kindness.

MEETING HENRY MOODY
THE TRUE STORY OF MRS. DILL
QUEEN GEORGE

Meeting Henry Moody

I met Henry Moody today. Mr. Wilson sent me to Armstrong's Book and Printing Shop on Queen Street to pick up some books he ordered. Henry came out of the back and looked me up and down like he was trying to decide if I was worth talking to. I think he decided that I wasn't. I think he thought he was better than me just because he was a town boy and I was from the country.

Boston is big. There are finely dressed people everywhere you look and the narrow, winding streets are noisy and crowded with traffic. Drivers of the ox-drawn wagons shout and crack their whips. Iron-tired wheels clank loudly on the cobblestones. Carts and chaises race down the twisted alleys and you have to keep a sharp watch while you dodge across. One time a fancy coach drawn by six white horses came within inches of running me down. Near the place where King, Queen, and Cornhill streets meet, that's the busiest place in town. I don't know what would have happened if I hadn't got behind that post in time.

After Henry finished inspecting me, he said, "State your business," taking off his steel-bound spectacles and cleaning them to show me he had more important things to do than talk to me. I asked if Mr. Armstrong was in. Mr. Wilson hadn't said anything to me about Henry. He said that Mr. Armstrong was upstairs in the printing shop setting type and getting the paper ready. I told him I had been sent by Mr. Wilson and had come to pick up some books he ordered.

"So you're the new boy," he said smartly. "I suppose I am," I said just as smartly. Then he told me to wait right there while he got the books. When he returned, he said to tell Mr. Wilson that two more were expected next week. I said I would and turned to leave. "Wait," he said, almost sounding friendly. He said he had heard how Mr. Wilson found me sleeping along the side of the road and how I was going to help Mrs. Thompson with the tavern, now that she was alone. Mr. Thompson left last year. Just picked up and disappeared, leaving Mrs. Thompson to see to the tavern and the baby all by herself. I wondered why he knew so much about me and came right out and asked him. It turns out Mr. Armstrong told him. Mr. Armstrong and Mr. Wilson are good friends, Henry explained. I asked him where he was from—you could tell by the way he talked that he wasn't from around here. He said he was from Liverpool. That's in England. And he has been working for

Mr. Armstrong for three years. He used to live with his uncle, but that didn't last. He came here when he was eleven. It took two awful months to cross the sea. He's fourteen now—two years older than me. He was telling me all this, but you could see that he still thought he was superior—talking to a mere country boy.

Henry asked me if I'd been to the burying grounds at Copp's Hill in the North End. He was pleased that I hadn't and wanted me to go with him. It seems to me that Henry has a gruff exterior but underneath he'd like a friend to do things with.

Burying grounds always give me the chills. Henry said they give him the chills, too, but we agreed to go even though it might be scary.

The night was clear, the stars were twinkling and the moon was full. We were lying on our backs, side by side with our heads resting on two headstones, and Henry asked me if I knew who Mrs. Dill was. I did and told him so.

He asked me if I knew the true story of what happened to her when she was younger and I said I didn't. Then Henry proceeded to tell me the true story of Mrs. Dill.

The True Story of Mrs. Dill

According to Henry, Mrs. Dill was captured by Indians many years ago, when she was just a young girl. The howling heathens, their hair smeared with bear grease and their bodies painted all over, had poured out of the forest in the middle of the night and swooped down on her village. They piled up hay and wood outside the houses and set them all on fire, roasting everyone alive except for her. She was spared because one of the savages wanted her for his bride, even though she was only fourteen and he already had a wife, as it turns out.

He pulled her up onto his horse and made her ride back to their camp, where she had no choice but to marry him.

She waited patiently for the right moment to escape. They forced her to eat dog flesh and follow their heathen habits. After a year the Indians began to think that she had given up all hope of seeing a white man again. After two years they treated her as a member of the tribe and her husband no longer took precautions to prevent her from escaping.

During that time she was befriended by the younger brother of her husband's other wife. He was now her husband's sworn secret enemy and offered to help. He had a plan, but it had to wait for the right time. When the time came, she was ready.

The Indian brave gave her poison, which she put in her

husband's drink that night, just before dawn. Once she was certain that the poison had worked, she crept out of their wigwam, stole away from the camp and made her way on foot back to her village.

I asked Henry how he knew this story and he said Mr. Armstrong had a book in his shop written by Mrs. Dill that tells of her years in captivity and her daring escape. That's where she gets all her money, Henry said, from the sales of her book. She doesn't use the name Dill on the book because she's pretty delicate now and doesn't want anyone to know about her past. Only Henry and Mr. Armstrong, and now me, know the true story. Not even Mr. Dill knows, according to Henry.

I was just about to ask him how he knew that Mrs. Dill, who doesn't look to me like she could poison anyone, is the same girl as the girl in the book, when all of a sudden Henry let out a howl that I feared might truly wake the dead. He jumped up and began running around and waving his arm in the air. At first I thought it was an Indian war dance that must have something to do with the story. But it went on for so long I began to fear that there was something wrong and so I decided to see what had Henry in such a state.

It didn't take long to find out. Slithering away in the moonlight was a good-sized snake that, I figured, must have just taken a chunk out of Henry's arm.

First things first, I thought, and pulled out one of the head-stones we had been leaning on and crushed the snake's head flatter than a pancake. Then I tried to get Henry to let me have a look at his arm, but he just kept running around in circles, waving his arm in the air and crying out in pain. I had to tackle him and pull him down to the ground so I could get a good look.

Henry is pretty fat and much bigger than me so I had quite a time wrestling him down. But I'm stronger than you would think just by looking at me and once I had him on the ground I was able to hold down his legs with my knees while I looked at his arm.

It was a snake bite all right. You could see that right off. I took out the knife Papa gave me for my birthday and began to cut open the skin around the bite. Once Henry realized what was happening he let out another one of those howls and tried to get up but I wouldn't let him. I put my hands on his shoulders and leaned down on him with all my weight and asked him if he wanted to see the sun rise in the morn-ing, but he was still looking around for what bit him and only quieted down when I got a stick and held the limp snake up in the air for him to see.

On the way back I made Henry keep his elbow bent and his fingers straight up, just like Papa taught me. When we finally got back to the tavern, Mrs. Thompson applied a plaster of turmeric root and told Henry to make sure he keeps it on.

I told Mrs. Thompson what Henry said about Mrs. Dill and she just laughed and said she couldn't wait to tell that to Mr. Wilson.

In the morning I had to run back to the cemetery to find Henry's spectacles, which we left behind in the commotion.

Henry no longer treats me like a simple country boy, and we are good and true friends.

This morning I applied a fresh coat of paint to the swinging sign that hangs outside above the door. It was badly in need of repainting. You could hardly see two of the stars. Mrs. Thompson told me to check the chains that held the wooden arm because last year a sign over at the Blue Bell Tavern blew down during a fierce winter storm and killed someone who was just walking by.

Sure enough one of the chains appeared in need of mending. Not wanting to take any chances, I took it over to Mr. Monk's to have it fixed. Mr. Monk is a blacksmith. He let me work the bellows, although I had to stand on a box to reach the handles.

Mr. Wilson was supposed to have a tooth drawn today but I think he is afraid because of what happened to Mrs. Paddock. Her jaw broke during an attempt to extract a bad tooth. Mrs. Paddock was in constant pain for some weeks.

He has not left his room all day. He hasn't even come down for his usual midday meal of boiled fish, bread and ale.

It's thanks to Mrs. Thompson that my letters are so good. From the first week I arrived she has insisted that I copy her rules of good behavior in a neat, firm hand.

This week's rules are:

* RISE EARLY.
* DO NOT BE LAZY WHILE DOING CHORES.
* BE DILIGENT WITH MY LEARNING.
* BE SLOW TO ANGER.
* DO NOT BLEND WORDS TOGETHER WHEN SPEAKING.

She's right about that. Sometimes I do talk so fast it's hard to understand what I am saying. That's what Mama always said, too.

Queen George

I carefully check Mrs. Thompson's list of chores to make sure I remember to do everything:

Sweep and scrub floors
Wash glasses and dishes
Empty and scrub chamber pots
Clean and fix candlesticks
Help wash and scrub clothes (Mondays)
and iron (Tuesdays)

I don't know how Mrs. Thompson does it. The water in the tub is boiling hot and she just puts her arms in it up to her elbows.

I keep an eye on Becca so she doesn't go near it. Fortunately, she minds me most of the time. She's almost two and is getting too big for her baby tender. She wants to walk on her own, although she can't quite. If you take your eyes off her, she's gone. Today I saw her just in time or rather heard her just in time. She was blowing her baby whistle and crawling like a crab, heading straight for the kettle of water. She must have climbed out when my head was turned, keeping track of the new puppy from Mr. Nelson. I don't want her to be scalded.

I wish Mrs. Thompson hadn't agreed to take one of Mr. Nelson's puppies in partial payment for his bill. Just because his dog had puppies doesn't mean we have to have one, as far as I'm concerned. Don't we have enough to do without that? I would have preferred if Mr. Nelson found some other way to pay off his bill. Bringing us a cake from his bakery, perhaps.

Now everything is turned even more upside down than usual. The puppy doesn't obey one command, can't be left unattended, and does its business everywhere but where it's supposed to. I must say, however, that it is as sweet a creature as I have ever known—all furry and black with sad, sorrowful brown eyes.

She's a Newfoundland. Mrs. Thompson said she'll be bigger than me soon.

Mr. Wilson said we ought to call her King George in honor of his royal majesty. But Mrs. Thompson reminded him that he's a she, so we have decided to name her Queen George.

The Burglar

Me and Henry stopped at Mr. Williams's shop on Cow Lane. He has clocks, watches and a whole collection of instruments for surveying: compasses, quadrants, protractors, scales, magnets and magnifying glasses. He also makes false teeth. Henry says they look just like natural teeth.

Mr. Williams doesn't mind if you look at things, as long as you are careful not to break them. He has a spyglass and said it would be all right if we wanted to take it outside and try it, which we did.

Everything looked close: The big British warships that fill the harbor looked like their cannons were pointed right at us. We saw some soldiers way in the distance, down by the docks, and we pretended we were secretly spying on them. We could even see their mouths move as they spoke. At times it appeared they had caught us spying on them, but we were too far away and they were just looking in our direction.

We didn't stay long because we were afraid we would miss the whipping. Jimmy Carr, Mr. Williams's apprentice, came with us. We ran most of the way, playing stone poison. I

21

tagged Jimmy first and he lost his balance and stepped on a stone. That made him mad and caused him to say he wouldn't play anymore. Henry doesn't like Jimmy Carr. He said he doesn't trust him.

On the way to the whipping post on King Street, we saw two unfortunate fellows who were hanging in the pillory with signs on them saying CHEATS. Their heads and hands were fitted into the holes and they had to stand in that hapless position and endure the jests and jibes of all those who passed by.

We hurried along because we could see that a crowd was already forming at the post. Fortunately there was enough room for us to be in the front. We wanted to make sure we got a good look at the burglar. They say he took some stockings that were in a shop window on Queen Street.

The wretched-looking man was wheeled out from the prison in a huge iron cage. He was then removed from the cage and tied to the red whipping post. I had brought a load of garbage from the tavern and we threw it at him before they started the whipping. I hit him right between the eyes with a rotten egg. Everyone cheered when I did that. Then forty lashes were applied to his bare back despite his screams, which were, at times, drowned out by the roar of the crowd calling for more.

I don't think he'll be taking what isn't rightly his anytime soon.

I told Mrs. Thompson all about it when I got back. She said it was high time they did something about all the stealing that's been going on. We lock all the doors at night because of it.

Henry says that's why Mr. Armstrong has him sleep in a cot in the back room. Mr. Armstrong says it's a good precaution to take because of the thieves that have been about. I was going to tell Henry that I didn't think any thieves would take the trouble to break into a bookshop where all they could steal is books, which are of little value to anyone unless you're going to read them. But I decided not to. Henry is very loyal to Mr. Armstrong and treats the books like they are precious jewels.

Mrs. Thompson said I did a good job with the provisions this time. Last week I forgot two things and had to go back, and it was too late. I left for the square as soon as I heard the bells. Mrs. Thompson said the market was going to close at noon today and to get there before the stalls become crowded and they run out. This has been happening a lot lately. Provisions are getting scarcer each week because the British have closed the harbor. Thankfully sheep from Connecticut, as well as corn, wheat, rice and barrels of flour, have recently arrived.

This week I was able to get only three of the items on Mrs. Thompson's list.

Provisions:

Cheese ✓
Butter
Eggs
Wheat
Flour
Turnips
Corn
Peas
Apples
Raisins
Pepper ✓
Nutmeg
Allspice
Cinnamon
Cloves ✓

As soon as I returned from the market, I had to take Becca to Mr. Monk to see if there was anything he could do about the stye in her eye. Mrs. Thompson has tried using a rotten apple, but the stye persists. Mr. Monk is glad to do anything Mrs. Thompson wants. When he's at the tavern, his eyes follow her everywhere.

It was no easy task taking Queen George and Becca all the way to Mr. Monk's. Queen George darted in and out of every alley in search of adventure or food, I wasn't sure which. Becca wriggled in my arms, attempting to climb down and walk, which was quite out of the question. Fortunately she's such a good-natured girl that when I decided to run the rest of the way, she giggled the whole time while Queen George brought up the rear.

Mr. Monk held Becca close to the flames of his fire—Becca let him because she likes him so much—and in no time the steamy heat broke the stye. She didn't even cry once. She's a strong girl, just like her mother. She was so happy when we got back. I put her in her go-cart and let her race around the barroom floor to her heart's content.

The Fitch Sisters and the Committee

Mrs. Thompson is still angry about the Fitch sisters, who have a shop on Milk Street. She never raises her voice like that.

"It's just like them to think they could bring in British goods and get away with it. You can count on the Fitch sisters to be concerned only about themselves, even in times like these. Imagine, claiming they are just trying to keep a roof over their heads and food on the table. Isn't that all any of us are doing?"

The Fitch sisters say that if they didn't have British goods to sell they would find themselves poor in no time. But Mrs. Thompson says they're only making it harder on themselves by defending their actions and they should just admit their mistake.

Mrs. Thompson has known the Fitch sisters since she was a little girl. She said she didn't like them much then either.

"They're just a pair of old maids and if that little one doesn't mind her tongue I'll take the other eye out and then she won't be able to see any of her precious British baubles."

One of the Fitch sisters, the short one, is blind in one eye.

"They ought to get the same treatment as Mr. Carlisle," Mrs. Thompson said.

Henry told me all about Mr. Carlisle. We saw him one day walking down King Street dressed in lace and ruffles. Henry said he has long been suspected of being loyal to the crown and one night he finally got what he deserved. Some of the men from town marched out to his house. Mr. Carlisle is very rich, Henry said, "Almost as rich as Mr. Dudley. Mr. Carlisle's house was one of the grandest in Boston."

As soon as the crowd arrived they trampled the lawn, hacked down the trees, and overran the gate that surrounds the house. They smashed the big front doors with axes and then poured into the house, where they tore up the floorboards, ripped the curtains from the windows and, after finding Mr. Carlisle's portrait, tore the eyes out.

They dragged his finely carved furniture outside and smashed it to bits, ran off with his carpets and drank his wine cellar dry.

They found Mr. Carlisle cowering upstairs, trying to hide behind his bed curtains. They pulled him out despite his feeble efforts to hold on to the bedpost and then took his feather bed and threw it out the window. A ladder was put up and Mr. Carlisle was lowered to those waiting below.

Once they had him outside, they stripped off his nightclothes, smeared him with hot tar and covered him with the insides of the feather bed.

When the house caught fire someone wanted to call for the firemen, but the crowd shouted him down, yelling, "LET IT BURN, LET IT BURN," and so they did. The flames, Henry said, could be seen for miles by dawn. When it was over, Mr. Carlisle's grand house had been reduced to a charred and smoldering skeleton.

Most of the men pulled nightcaps over their heads or darkened their faces with chimney soot so they wouldn't be recognized. Some were armed with sticks and clubs and Henry said that Mr. Carlisle was lucky not to have suffered even greater injury to his person than to his pride.

Of course, Mrs. Thompson didn't say any of this to me. I overheard it when she was talking to Mr. Wilson right before he went into the regular Tuesday night meeting with the Committee.

That's why I stay put on Tuesday nights. I never go anywhere. They meet late, after the tavern closes, in the small room next to the big barroom. As soon as I hear them all coming in I just lie there quietly on my cot and listen. The room is right over my head. Directly above where I sleep. The cracks in the floor are so wide that I can hear everything that goes on. And there's an awful lot that goes on lately.

They were all there: Mr. Wilson; Mr. Cummings—he's a merchant; Dr. Endicott; Mr. Palmer, who is a lawyer; Mr. Armstrong; Mr. Davis, the barber, who doesn't say much; and Mr. Monk.

Tonight they talked about the Fitch sisters and what is to be done.

Mr. Cummings said anyone found bringing in goods from the "mother country" should be punished swiftly and harshly. You could tell by the way he said "mother country" that he didn't mean it nicely. He wants to place a wooden post with a hand pointed toward their shop as a warning not to buy from them.

Mr. Palmer said that buying from England is "giving aid to the enemy, plain and simple." Mr. Palmer is of an ardent temperament and the most talkative man alive. He's quite quick-tempered and sometimes gets so excited, his jaw twitches and he stutters. I think it's because he has too much spit in his mouth when he talks.

Mr. Armstrong said they should proceed with caution because "we don't want to turn our own against us." Mr. Armstrong is calm and good-natured—a fair-spoken and fine gentlemen. But, he warned, if they do not mend their ways perhaps a visit from the Committee would be called for.

As far as I could tell, Mr. Wilson was just listening quietly the whole time. I did not hear him speak once. Mr. Wilson likes to choose his words carefully—like he was paying a high price for each one.

Mr. Wilson's article about the Fitch sisters appeared in the *Gazette* this week. He is a powerful writer.

BRITISH BAUBLES

*W*E MUST all learn to do without British baubles—shopkeepers and patrons alike. To become a VIRTUOUS people, we must begin to act in a VIRTUOUS manner.

WE MUST be willing to *SACRIFICE* conveniences and endure hardship. Liberty is a precious commodity—it will not be achieved easily. Although our cause is just, we will not triumph without unity.

WE MUST *ALL* pull together. One heart, one mind. OUR UNION IS OUR STRENGTH.

SOME SAY Martha and Tabitha FITCH are LOYALISTS, but we say no. They are simply *INNOCENT VICTIMS* caught in the middle and forced by circumstances not of their own making to face an uncertain future. Innocent victims who have made an error in judgment, nothing more.

WE ADVISE them to *CEASE* their grievous and regrettable activities and discontinue their misguided ways.

WE URGE them to consider this *FAIR WARNING*.

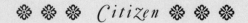

❋ ❋ ❋ *Citizen* ❋ ❋ ❋

It took me all morning to clean the candlesticks. First I had to go around and make sure I found all of them. Sometimes the candlesticks are left where I can't find them, which makes my work that much harder. Last week I forgot to check the back room and had to do them late at night. I always try to do the candles in the morning. I clean off all the unburned tallow and remove any that are too short to last the evening. When I am done I put them in a tin box I keep in the pantry. That is so the mice won't get them. It's also a handy place, so everyone knows where to find them when nighttime comes.

The barroom was crowded today as everyone was waiting for Mr. Wilson to return with the papers. All are eager to hear what is being said in London about our present circumstances.

OUR SPOILED CHILDREN who live across the vast ocean must be punished for their outrageous behavior and their violent and unforgivable ACTS OF TREASON. They must be taught that they too are subject to the laws of PARLIAMENT and the will of the KING and that subverting his majesty's just Government and willfully destroying the public tranquility cannot and will not be tolerated.
The Massachusetts Bay Colony is nothing more than a nest of vipers led by indolent and insolent men who have nothing to lose.

THEY MUST BE MADE AN EXAMPLE OF.

Not only should the Port of BOSTON remain closed, but its rebellious inhabitants placed under MILITARY RULE until they come to their senses.

Today is Becca's birthday. Mrs. Thompson made her a blueberry pie, which is her favorite. I think that's because it makes the best mess. Mr. Monk gave her a tea set he fashioned, Mr. Armstrong a miniature leatherbound book, Mrs. Paddock and Mrs. Dill a gingerbread house they made and Mr. Wilson a waxed doll. I think Becca had a good time.

Down at the Docks

Henry and me went down to the Long Wharf and played pitch penny. It was nearly deserted now that the British have closed the port. None of our ships can come or go. The only vessels are their warships, sitting in the harbor riding their moving chains—cannons pointed menacingly toward the town.

Time was, Henry said, before this summer and all the trouble started, that the docks were alive with sailors in their black-brimmed hats and blue bell trousers. Back then, he says, the ships were constantly discharging their catches and cargoes onto the docks. The workmen were kept busy rolling barrels down the planks and pushing their loaded carts into the warehouses and shops along the Long Wharf.

Now, many of the shops have closed because business is so poor.

It was so hot, we just stripped off our clothes. I jumped in and swam all the way out to where the British fort is. It must be two miles to Castle Island, maybe more. I'm a good swimmer. Papa said he taught me to swim before I could walk, but Mama told me that wasn't entirely true.

Henry waited on the dock. He can't swim and besides he was afraid he would get into trouble. Henry said Mr. Armstrong warned him to stay clear of the lobsterbacks. Back in England, he said, they get unsuspecting men drunk, shove a shilling in their palms and, when they wake up in the morning, they discover they're British soldiers for the next seven years. Most of them, Mr. Armstrong said, are the sweepings from England's jails and are not to be trifled with. Mr. Armstrong hates the British nearly as much as Mr. Wilson does. They're good friends, those two.

Mr. Armstrong is right about the soldiers, but Henry has a rambling imagination and works himself into a state about the smallest matter.

Last night, being Tuesday, the Committee met and talked until late about the closing of the harbor.

Dr. Endicott said the blockade was already taking a toll. The sailors have no work and many businesses are suffering. People are in a distressed state. He said the British will not rest until they have made us pay for dumping their precious tea. They will keep the port closed to all seagoing traffic until they have their money and we have given up our resistance to their rule.

Mr. Cummings interrupted and said, "If we let them tax our tea, the next thing we know they'll tax the sunlight that brightens our day and the water that quenches our thirst. If they're waiting for us to surrender our rights because we fear being starved into submission by their sinister blockade, then we must let them know that the port can remain closed for all eternity."

When he said that, everyone cheered. Mr. Cummings is a rousing speaker—he speaks as well as Mr. Wilson writes.

Keeping Accounts

Mrs. Thompson asked me to take an inventory of all the things in the cellar. She said she couldn't remember the last time anyone went through all of it.

Inventory:

5	bottles sherry		lime juice
3	bottles apple brandy		bitters
			cinnamon water
3	bottles Madeira		clove water
2	bottles peach brandy		mint water
			punch bowls
15	gallons rum		decanters
17	gallons cider		tumblers
	beer		funnels
	ale		nutmeg grater

I had to straighten everything out before I could even begin. It took me all night and the better part of the next day just to get things in order. When I was done, nothing was in the same place it had been when I started. I just finished the list last night. I would have finished it in half the time if I hadn't had Becca with me. She did have a good time, I'll say that. I wasn't watching as closely as I should have and she and Queen George got into an empty barrel that must have been lying on its side. When I turned around to see what all the noise was about, this barrel, barking and laughing, came rolling across the floor at me. I stopped it with my foot and dumped the two of them out, which resulted in even greater squealing. Queen George is almost as big as Becca now. I was surprised the two of them could fit in the barrel.

Mr. Wilson wants me to help Mrs. Thompson keep the tavern's account book. He showed me the desk in the corner next to the bar where it is kept. There's a quill box and ink horn on it that Mr. Wilson uses.

He raised the slanting top and showed me how to calculate anyone's bill that is over thirty days old. But, he said, I had to be sure not to mention that to Mrs. Thompson. If she knew, she would not allow it.

Mr. Wilson said that if we don't find a way to get Mrs. Thompson out of the hole she's in, we'll have to look elsewhere for our lodgings. The tavern, he said, is close to financial ruin.

I can tell from the account book that Mr. Thompson left Mrs. Thompson with a long list of people who owe the tavern money.

Mr. Wilson and Mrs. Thompson have even talked about moving to another location where business might be better. Business is better at the British Coffee House—down by the Long Wharf—that's where all the loyalists go.

Mrs. Thompson says that if we move she would have to find new patrons and start all over again and that's too risky.

But Mr. Wilson thinks they will all follow Mrs. Thompson wherever she goes. I think Mr. Wilson is right about that. She treats everyone with such courtesy—even those who don't deserve it.

Mr. Wilson says that Mrs. Thompson is too generous. "Generosity," he said, "is usually a trait I admire but given the greatness of the rent and the meagerness of the business, either our generosity has to diminish or we do."

He told me sternly that I should be dunning in the strictest manner.

I think Mrs. Thompson should be more like Mr. Williams. He sells only for cash. He has a sign up as soon as you walk in his shop, plain as day:

> *Time's up – I can play no more*
> *I trusted once and I've trusted before*
> *But if justice be served I can trust no more*
> *So pay up or walk out the door.*
> *— J. Williams*

Mrs. Thompson is hoping that coffee will help. Once tea was all anyone drank, but now no one does, unless they want to be considered a traitor to their country. Coffee is becoming fashionable with the better sort. That's what Mrs. Thompson says. If you ask me it's more trouble than it's worth. I have to mill it right in the barroom and as if there wasn't enough to do already I have to keep track of cups and dishes just for coffee.

Mr. Wilson says there are just too many taverns on King Street and too little money.

I would like us to stay where we are. I'm so tired of moving about. It would be best if everyone would just pay Mrs. Thompson what they owe her and our worries would be over.

Mrs. Thompson let Mr. Bacon, the hatter on Newbury

Street, pay her in beaver hats. Now he owes us nothing and we have seven beaver hats. This seems foolish to me. The hats, all seven of them, are still down in the cellar. I tried one on when I was cleaning up. I admit they're nice but I don't see that they will do us much good.

In the morning, when it's first light, I go over the account book so I can be ready when Mr. Wilson needs me to do it on my own.

The Goal of Every Patriot

Mr. Wilson took me with him to Mr. Davis's. Mr. Davis fought in the French and Indian War. He is good with a knife or a gun. Last year he killed a bear two miles outside of Boston. He is a man who can be counted on in a pinch, Mr. Wilson says.

Mr. Davis provided to the patriot cause flints, muskets, powder horns and lead balls, which he casts in the kitchen.

"It must be the goal of every patriot to be certain his bullet finds the target," Mr. Wilson said. By "target" he means the British soldiers. If it comes to fighting, Mr. Wilson said, fire at the ones with the reddest coats because they are the officers and it's best that they die first.

I can hit a bull's-eye pretty regularly but my rate of firing is not as good. "Better to be sure than quick," Mr. Wilson said. Mr. Davis said I handled myself real good. I told him I used to go rabbit hunting with Papa in the woods back of the barn.

Henry's Studious Countenance

Henry likes being Mr. Armstrong's apprentice. He was fortunate, he said. If not for Mr. Armstrong he doesn't know what would have become of him.

When Henry's ship docked, Mr. Armstrong was one of the last to come on board to see who was being offered for sale. Henry had already been passed over by the others because he looked so ill from the two-month ocean voyage. He says that Mr. Armstrong picked him because he was sorry for him. Henry says Mr. Armstrong laughs every time he tells him that's what he thought. He told Henry that the reason he picked him was because he had such a "studious countenance," which he does, in large part because of his spectacles. Henry tutors Samuel and Nathaniel, Mr. Armstrong's twin boys. He takes his responsibilities with the boys quite seriously. They're only eight but already Henry has them on the road to scholarly studies. Mr. Armstrong told him how pleased he is but Henry still thinks Mr. Armstrong took him because he was sorry for him. Once Henry convinces himself of something, there's no use trying to change his mind.

After Henry and Mr. Armstrong agreed on his length of service—six years—Mr. Armstrong paid the captain the money for passage Henry owed. Henry had no choice but to come here after his uncle threw him on the cold mercies of the world. Of course, he had no money of his own because his uncle refused to forward him any.

Mrs. Armstrong provides him with sufficient meat, drink and clothes, and Mr. Armstrong is teaching him how to arrange the books on the shelves according to category: the classics, military books, spelling and schoolbooks, almanacs and pamphlets.

Henry said he is also learning printing. Every Friday he is busy all day helping Mr. Armstrong set the type so the paper can be ready on Monday. This week's edition is four full pages long, Henry said proudly.

He's a clever boy, Henry.

Spent most of the day whitewashing the tavern walls. It is tedious work but Mrs. Thompson is right, it does look nice. I think it is a good sign. That means we won't be moving.

Becca will soon be walking on her own. She's getting too big for her go-cart. As soon as I put her in it she gets fidgety and won't rest until I take her out.

One thing I wish Mrs. Thompson wouldn't make me do is dip Becca in the barrel of cold water every morning. I know it's good for her but she howls like a savage until I stop. I don't think she likes it much.

Mrs. Thompson said I was doing a good job with Becca. She said that you usually can't count on boys to be good with babies. She asked me where I learned to care for a child so well. I told her my sister was born when I was five and I helped Mama care for her right from the start.

I didn't tell Mrs. Thompson that my sister's name was Becca, too.

◆━◆

Mr. Davis and the Loud Man

Mr. Davis was sitting with Dr. Endicott and Mr. Monk, as usual. Another man who I had never seen before joined them. I didn't take much notice at first because I was so busy helping Mrs. Thompson, who had her hands full tending bar. It must be that everyone's so thirsty because of the heat.

The man I had never seen before was doing all of the talking and the more he talked the thirstier he got, and the more he drank the louder he talked. Mr. Davis was just listening, leaning back so his chair was balanced on the hind two legs and just staring at the man, slowly drinking his ale, just like he always does.

I could see that Mr. Davis was getting hotter by the word. I don't think the loud man realized that Mr. Davis was staring at him and he just went right on talking in this loud, booming voice that you could hear even above the chatter and clatter that is all about.

Then, suddenly, out of the corner of my eye I saw something flash in the flickering candlelight, and the next thing I knew the loud man was lying on the floor, his shirt and breeches drenched in blood, clutching his stomach and groaning dismally.

Dr. Endicott and Mr. Monk jumped to their feet and carried him out the door and down to Dr. Endicott's office.

Mr. Davis didn't say a thing. He just sat back down, cleaned his knife blade on his pants, put it back in his boot and asked politely as ever if he could trouble me for another ale, which I brought him in the wink of an eye.

When Mr. Monk returned, he said that the man didn't look like he was hurt too bad, although he did lose a lot of blood. Dr. Endicott guessed he would probably make it. Mr. Monk said that the man was distempered with drink and the next time perhaps he would do his drinking at the British Coffee House with the other loyalists.

I don't know what the loud man said to Mr. Davis that got him so angry, and I don't like spreading rumors, but I overheard Mrs. Paddock saying that the man said something about Molly, Mr. Davis's daughter. Of course everyone has seen Molly with that British soldier. The one that works at the warehouse when he's off duty. But no one is foolish enough to say anything to Mr. Davis about it. Mr. Davis looks after Molly like a mother hen, especially since Mrs. Davis died.

Mr. Davis was back the next night drinking his ale slow as ever and sitting with Dr. Endicott and Mr. Monk same as if nothing had happened.

My Time Will Come

Mr. Wilson is always so busy writing his articles, working on his pamphlets and meeting with the Committee.

I told him I wanted to help and he said I already was by helping Mrs. Thompson.

I told him I was hoping to be called upon for something a little more important than keeping the account book and one eye on Becca and one on Queen George's ever more frequent coming and goings.

This gave Mr. Wilson a good laugh. Mr. Wilson is a serious man but he still likes a good laugh now and again.

"Be patient, son," he said. "Your time will come, perhaps sooner than you'd like."

Then he paused, clasped his hands together like he was about to pray and bent his head down till his lips touched the tips of his fingers. I have learned that is always a sign that Mr. Wilson is giving something the utmost concentration and that it is best not to interrupt him, so I remained silently where I stood.

"Perhaps," he said, "I do have a little job for you, Will."

He gave me a handbill he had written urging the British soldiers to desert. Some, Mr. Wilson said, desert just as soon as they get here, thirty in the first two weeks, but the others have to be convinced. He asked me to take it to Mr. Armstrong and wait while he prints them.

It was late and I feared Mr. Armstrong would be asleep. Mr. Wilson told me to wake him up and tell him to make a quick job of it. He warned me, however, to be careful on the way back and to not let any lobsterbacks see me with the handbills. If they do, they might get angry. The British are eager to catch anyone who suggests they desert.

LAND OF OPPORTUNITY

*C*ROSS the line, boys.

Show us WHICH SIDE you're on.

JOIN US . . . tradesman, hunter, plain folk, tiller of the soil.

ALL ARE WELCOME.

Here, in our PROSPEROUS towns, there is a place for you.

Here, where land is PLENTIFUL, there is room for you.

Here, where there are GOOD PAYING jobs, there is opportunity for you.

Here, there is a BETTER LIFE for you.

Come to where liberty reigns and NOT the KING.

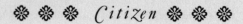

❀ ❀ ❀ *Citizen* ❀ ❀ ❀

Mrs. Paddock Orders a Flip

Mrs. Paddock is getting fatter by the day. Her face is so red I keep thinking I'll hear an explosion any time now and learn the sad news that she has finally burst into pieces.

She smells, too. If you ask me it's from the oil she uses to make the powder stick on her hair. It's a mystery to me how she gets it to stand so high.

She always calls me "boy" no matter how many times I tell her my name is Will. William Thomas Emerson, I tell her, but it doesn't do any good. She said that William Thomas Emerson is a distinguished name and I was right to be proud of it.

She was in her favorite seat, the one by the window, talking to Mrs. Dill. Last week there was someone sitting there when she and Mrs. Dill came in and she just walked right up to him and asked him to be so kind as to take another chair. That's her in a nutshell.

I was trying to pretend she wasn't there, but she hooked my arm as I walked past her. "Be a darling boy and bring me my flip," she said. I've decided not to waste any more time trying to get her to use my rightful name. Some people don't listen to a thing you say no matter how many times you say it and Mrs. Paddock is surely one of them. Mrs. Thompson says Mrs. Paddock's just a step away from a good-for-nothing—she's good for little.

She asked if I was sure I knew how to prepare a flip properly.

I wasn't certain but I didn't tell her that. I told her that I was. She said to make sure there was plenty of rum and that the poker was sufficiently hot before I stuck it in so that it bubbled and foamed real good.

I had to ask Mrs. Thompson to show me one more time. I watched closely and tried to remember everything: two thirds beer, egg, some molasses, dried pumpkin and rum. I made sure the poker was real hot before I stuck it in and then I stirred it till it was thick. I don't know why people want to drink something that tastes like burnt iron.

The tankard of flip is so big that it is the only thing I can carry to the table for fear of spilling some. I had to come back to the barroom for Mrs. Dill's cider.

Mrs. Paddock and Mrs. Dill were having one of their more spirited conversations. They're quite a pair. Mrs. Dill's as thin as Mrs. Paddock's fat and as quiet as she's not. I suppose they're company for each other because Mrs. Dill is such a good listener and Mrs. Paddock such a good talker.

Ever since Henry told me that story I keep looking at Mrs. Dill to see if I can see anything. Sometimes she catches me looking, and I wonder if she knows why.

I couldn't hear what they were talking about, although I tried as hard as I could to lean over each time I passed their table.

Poor Mr. Paddock sat in the corner looking over his bills and carefully reading the newspaper with a worried look on his face. I think he keeps rereading the newspaper because he's afraid he might miss something important. These days he just might. There's something happening every time you turn around.

Henry said that Mr. Paddock came down with a nervous fever some years ago. He was subject to the most violent fits and was teetering on the edge of madness when he was bound and taken to a farm outside of Boston. He was locked in an attic until his disordered mind finally found some peace. Although he's still demented, Henry said he's not dangerous. He waits patiently for Mr. Nelson to come so that they can begin their evening chess game.

I never ask Mr. Paddock for money because Mrs. Thompson says he has fallen on hard times and cannot meet his obligations. She's sure he'll pay just as soon as he can. Mr. Paddock's a carpenter and, according to Henry, a good one. He's fixing one of our chairs.

He fell asleep again tonight. Every time Mrs. Paddock wakes him to take him home he says the same thing to her: "Mrs. Thompson serves the best rum in Boston, Mary, make no mistake. The best." He always says it just that way, no matter how much he drinks and no matter how long he sleeps. He never changes a word.

Mr. Palmer was playing darts with Mr. Williams. He has to throw with his left arm because he has no right arm.

Henry says he knows what happened. He says that when

Mr. Palmer was a boy a great boulder rolled on top of his right arm and crushed it till it was as thin as paper. His father had to cut it off with a handsaw and use a red-hot tong to stop the bleeding, which was considerable. He saved the boy's life but the arm was gone forever. I asked Henry how he knew this and he said that Mr. Armstrong told him. Sometimes, though, he doesn't separate what's true from what's fanciful. That's why I like to be with Henry. He sees things differently from most people. I told him he ought to write some of these stories down, but he just laughed and said that would be a waste of time.

Mr. Davis Brings a Salmon

Mr. Davis brought a freshly caught salmon, which Mrs. Thompson cooked for supper with corn and peas. He also brought Molly.

I tried to watch my table manners because Mrs. Thompson has recently remarked on them. "They could stand some improvement," according to her.

She taught me to: break off my bread and not just bite into it; wipe my knife before putting it in the salt and lay it down with the blade resting on the right-hand side of the plate; not eat so vastly and make less noise.

Unfortunately, I made the mistake of letting Queen George lick my spoon clean. Mrs. Thompson scolded me so that all assembled could hear.

My face was glowing like a furnace because Molly was laughing, which she said was because of the satisfied look on Queen George's furry face, but I'm not certain that was the true reason for her merriment.

They Look Big to Me

There was another serious fracas last night between the North End boys and the lobsterbacks. The soldiers were off duty acting rude and boisterous like they usually do and one of the North End boys grabbed a cobblestone and got one of them right behind the ear. The soldiers started throwing back and one thing led to another.

Boston looks more like a military garrison than a town with each passing day. There are more of them than there are of us. They drill all day long. You can hear the sound of the fife and drum for miles and the large wooden wheels of their field guns make a horrible racket on the cobblestone streets. The lobsterbacks jostle you when they walk past and, if you're not careful, they'll poke you in the ribs with the buttends of their bayonets just for a laugh. At night, they are often heated with liquor.

They are much taller than we are, although Mr. Wilson says it is only because of their hats. Perhaps that is true but I watch them strutting down our streets in their bright red coats, their bayonets glinting in the morning sun, and they look big to me. "You couldn't ask for a better target," Mr. Wilson says.

The new British general has them strengthening the defenses around town and at the Neck, where they are building a fort. They fear the patriots in the countryside will soon attack. They use Negro slaves to do all the hard work. No one will work for them. Mr. Paddock and the other carpenters won't help them build their barracks on the Common, even though they need the work and no lumber is being allowed in. Others refuse to sell them tools, blankets or goods of any kind.

Me, Henry and Jimmy Carr went down to the Common, where the lobsterbacks' white tents are pitched. They are camped all over, forcing the poor cows to look elsewhere for proper grazing. Still others are on Fort Hill and the Neck. We watched them take target practice and not one of them could hit the figures that stood stock-still before them. I could readily imagine how bad it would be if they were moving. Mr. Wilson's right—they'll be no match for patriot marksmen. Jimmy Carr yelled to one of the soldiers that he knew someone who could shoot the seeds out of an apple thrown into the air before it hit the ground, meaning Mr. Davis. The lobsterback laughed and told Jimmy to produce such a man. Jimmy said he would return before evening.

Later I told Mr. Davis but he didn't think it was so funny.

He was not pleased that we were taunting the soldiers. "Someone's gonna get hurt, if this doesn't stop," he said.

Fall 1774

BRINGING BOOKS TO ARMSTRONG'S
THE DIFFERENCE BETWEEN DOGS AND MEN
MY CONVERSATION WITH MR. WILSON
THE SANDS OF TIME ARE RUNNING OUT

Bringing Books to Armstrong's

Mr. Wilson gave me some books to bring back to Armstrong's and a list of others I am to return with. He reminded me to be sure to give the books only to Mr. Armstrong and no one else. "Not even your friend Henry," he said.

Henry thinks there is a note secreted in one of the books. A note written in milk so that the writing is invisible—that's what Henry thinks. The last time I brought some over, Henry wanted to look for the note, but I wouldn't let him. If Mr. Wilson wanted me to read a note, he would have said so. Henry said Mr. Armstrong now sleeps with a firearm by his side.

On the way I stopped at Nelson's Bakery on Crooked Lane. Mrs. Nelson gave me a plum cake, which I ate right off, and some rock candy, which I stuffed into my pockets for later. I was careful to thank Mrs. Nelson politely, just as Mrs. Thompson taught me. I am not sure if she heard me, however, she was so busy looking after her three little girls.

Mr. Armstrong was there when I arrived, but not Henry. He

had gone to see Mr. Paddock about some shelves he was making for the shop. Mr. Paddock brought the chair he was mending back yesterday. He did a fine job and I have credited his account accordingly. He has also promised to build a table and a corner cupboard for the pantry. Then his bill will be paid in full. Mrs. Thompson is pleased because the table is sorely needed and we do not have any money to pay for one. Frankly, I think we did better with Mr. Paddock than we did with Mr. Bacon's beaver hats.

Mr. Armstrong took the books and the list and said he wouldn't be long. He went into the back room. I looked around at the books and the magazines. I like looking around Mr. Armstrong's but not as much as I like looking at all the things in Mr. Williams's shop.

Another brawl broke out yesterday between the lobsterbacks and some sailors down at the Long Wharf. Later that same night the same bunch of soldiers, inflamed with rum and wine, smashed the new street lamps.

Mr. Wilson is still sleeping. He didn't rise yesterday until eight o'clock—a lazy hour. He has just returned on the stage. He complained all day about the journey, which he said was most uncomfortable and tedious. Mr. Wilson likes to be at home and is not one for traveling. He said he was coated with dust from head to toe because he refused to pay extra to ride in the coach and had to ride on top. The inn they stopped at along the way was crowded with travelers, so he was forced to share a bed with one of his companions—something he dislikes.

Mrs. Thompson told him he shouldn't complain because it's much warmer and safer to have someone share your bed. Mr. Wilson didn't seem to agree.

Everyone is talking about the soldier.

Two days ago the British recaptured a deserter. They marched him before a firing squad. A chaplain walked beside him, reading psalms aloud while a lone drummer beat his drum. After they shot him, the officer placed a white shroud over him and made the soldiers walk past his lifeless body, now lying in a pool of blood. This was done so that they might think twice before deserting themselves.

The Fitch sisters are gone. Their shop is closed and no one is there.

The Difference Between Dogs and Men

Mrs. Thompson hurt her wrist badly. She was down in the cellar getting some cider and she tripped over Queen George, who was not supposed to be down there. No one knew she was in the cellar—we thought she was out somewhere. She must have snuck in. Queen George's as fast as a cat and as quiet as a mouse even though she's already bigger than Becca.

Mrs. Thompson fell over her and, it is feared, fractured a bone. Thankfully it is not poking through her skin.

It is hard to see down in the cellar because the tiny windows let in little light and even that is blocked by the floor-to-ceiling shelves filled with cartons and crates.

Dr. Endicott explained his plan for a remedy and cautioned that it might be painful. He offered Mrs. Thompson something but she preferred not to cloud her mind and asked him to proceed without further discussion.

Dr. Endicott gripped Mrs. Thompson's arm and forced her swollen hand this way and that, causing a sound like the breaking of twigs in a dry forest to be heard. Mrs. Thompson's face gave no indication of the great discomfort she must have been feeling, other than a fixed set to the jaw and a paleness of complexion unlike her usual rosy glow.

After some hours of intense suffering, Mrs. Thompson lay down for a rest while I watched Becca and the tavern. Queen George insisted on lying beside her on the bed and would not be persuaded otherwise.

"Dogs are faithful, Will. It's men who are not," she said before she slept.

A British soldier drowned at Rowe's Wharf yesterday morning. He was on sentry duty and a little girl crawled off the end of the pier and fell in. She was going under and her mother was shrieking, "Help, help my little girl, my little girl," so the soldier jumped in and saved her but had no strength left to save himself and lost his life in the process.

The little Negro sweep came by today to clean the chimney. He's always singing that same sad song and looking at me with those same sad eyes. This time I was sure he had something he wanted to tell me. But just when I thought he was about to speak up, he turned away like he'd thought better of it.

He started up singing his song again while he swept the soot up into his blanket and didn't even glance at me once before he carted it away.

Mrs. Thompson wants to make sure he does a good job because sooty chimneys have caused many fires in recent years.

After many days Mrs. Thompson's wrist is nearly mended. We had my penmanship lesson today and she says that I am improving. Keeping my journal has helped but I didn't want to say anything about that to her, especially after my conversation last night with Mr. Wilson.

My Conversation with Mr. Wilson

Mr. Wilson said that it was most important not to tell anyone about our talk or anything that has to do with the activities of the Committee—not even Mrs. Thompson or Henry. He could see what I was thinking. It's not that he doesn't trust

Henry or Mrs. Thompson, just that at times like these, trust carries a dear price and you must err on the side of caution. The less said the better, Mr. Wilson warned, and I agree.

He said that he has observed me carefully since I came to work at the tavern. He said he thought I was a boy who could be trusted. A boy who could be counted on in a pinch.

He is aware that I can hear everything that goes on during the Tuesday night meetings and he knows that I have never betrayed him.

I asked him how he knew this and he laughed. "There is no need to go into details," he said. Certain things had been discussed at the meeting purely to test me. To see if I was a true patriot.

He asked, "Are you ready for your first assignment, William Thomas Emerson?"

"I am, sir," I replied.

The Sands of Time Are Running Out

Tomorrow night I am to help a British soldier desert. This on the heels of the most recent execution on the Common. Mr. Wilson could see I was thinking about that and he said I didn't have to do it if I didn't want to. I could wait, he said, for another assignment. I told him I didn't want to wait.

He'll be taken from the British barracks on the Common to the corner of Frog Lane and Orange Street at precisely nine o'clock.

The patriot accompanying the soldier, Mr. Wilson explained, is someone I can trust. All I have to do is walk up to them and say, "The sands of time are running out" and if everything is going according to plan, they will counter by saying, "It's time to choose and not to doubt," and hand the soldier over to me.

Mr. Wilson asked me if I could remember and to show him I repeated it.

He took a map out of his pocket, unfolded it, placed it on the table and flattened it out. He motioned for me to come sit beside him on the bench and pulled the candle closer. He showed me the corner where I was to meet the soldier and the other man and then, with his finger, he followed the route I should take to get from there to the Charles River, where a boat would be waiting. He cautioned that I not stray from the route. The Committee had chosen it because they considered it the safest.

He said it was good that I was familiar with Boston's narrow and twisted streets because they can lead nowhere and come out where you'd least expect them to. I assured him that I have been down every alley and taken every cutoff in Boston. "I know you have," Mr. Wilson said.

I am to take a change of clothes for the soldier and some cloth to muffle the thole pins, which hold the oars, lest their jangling give us away. I am to accompany him as far as the boat and no farther. The soldier knows how to get to Cambridge, Mr. Wilson said. People will be waiting there who will see to it that he is taken care of.

Mr. Wilson asked if I would be willing to do all that. I said I was, and he asked if I was scared and I said I wasn't.

Then Mr. Wilson looked at me with that squinty-eyed look he gets when he thinks something is even more important than usual. "I don't guess you are, Will, I don't guess you are," he said.

I thought we were done but we weren't. Although Mr. Wilson is a man of few words he had more to say.

"This is an exremely important assignment, Will. It would be important if it was just a British soldier who believed in our cause and wished not to fight against us in our upcoming struggle. But this soldier is more than that. He possesses special knowledge about military training, and once you help him get to Cambridge, he will be taken from there to teach our patriots proper military methods and maneuvers. By helping him now, you will be saving many lives in the future."

Yesterday couldn't go by quickly enough. At night I just lay there waiting. I left noiselessly, as I didn't know if Mrs. Thompson was aware of my mission.

I must have been early. When I got to the corner no one was there. I decided to wait across the street, where I backed into the darkness of a deserted doorway.

After only a few minutes I heard the church clock chime nine times. Then two people came down Frog Lane, right toward me, their footsteps echoing louder and louder in the stillness. They were almost on top of me and then they were past me. They stopped and stood right where Mr. Wilson said they would and waited. A short man and a taller one, who must have been the soldier.

I went over everything Mr. Wilson had said and walked toward them, stopping before I got too close.

"The sands of time are running out," I said, barely above a whisper. The short man replied, "It's time to choose and not to doubt."

I was so startled I couldn't move. It was a girl. "It's time to choose and not to doubt," she repeated, seeing that I was making no move to come closer. I was rooted to the spot.

It was Molly Davis, Mr. Davis's daughter, and, I now realized, standing next to her was the British soldier the loud man had been talking about. I came closer. It *was* Molly. She turned to the soldier but said nothing and was gone, leaving the two of us facing each other.

"Come with me," I said, hoping to sound older than I looked. It didn't work, though. The soldier asked me how old I was. Twelve, I told him. He said nothing as we followed the route that I now knew by heart, staying close to the buildings.

"Why are you doing this?" I asked, surprising both of us. It was something I had been thinking about but had no intention of asking. The words just jumped out before I realized what I was saying.

The soldier stopped, turned and put his hands on my shoulders. He asked if I wanted the truth or just a string of sweet-sounding words. "The truth," I answered although I wasn't at all certain.

"The truth," the soldier said, "is that I get paid little, eat poorly and am punished frequently and severely.

"But," he said, gripping my shoulders tighter and bringing his face so close I could smell him. "I wouldn't desert if it were for that alone." Then he stopped and looked at me, like he was making some kind of important judgment, his steady gray-eyed gaze sending shivers up and down my spine.

"The real truth is that the most important decision a man can make in his whole life is what he is willing to die for," and then he took his hands off my shoulders and said we'd better get where we were going.

As we continued along, we saw no one and encountered no difficulties.

The boat was just where Mr. Wilson had said it would be.

I kept it steady while the soldier stepped in. I handed him the bundle of clothes, stuffed the cloths into the thole pins and fought back the urge to ask him just one more question.

The soldier sat down cautiously, took the oars and, aided by a shove from my boot, rowed away from the shore toward Cambridge.

I stood there longer than I should have, straining to see the soldier in the little rowboat long after he had disappeared into the inky blackness. Even after I could no longer see him, I could still hear the soft splash as the oars entered the water. And then there was nothing.

✦╍✦

Mr. Monk Plays with Mrs. Thompson

Mr. Monk came in with his fiddle last night and he and Mrs. Thompson played some duets. I had no idea Mrs. Thompson could play the flute so nicely.

We had quite a crowd before the evening was over. People kept coming in all night long, hearing the music as they passed. The tavern was filled.

I didn't think I could keep up while Mrs. Thompson was playing, but Mr. Wilson tended bar and Mr. Davis and Molly brought drinks to the tables.

Everyone was laughing uproariously as they were all well supplied with strong drink. Mr. Paddock drank more than his share, slid under the table and was fast asleep most of the evening. There was so much smoke you couldn't see from one end of the barroom to the other.

A couple of sailors joined the fun. You could tell they were sailors because of the way they swung their arms when they walked. One of them was as dizzy as a goose.

Mr. Palmer offered a number of patriotic toasts, insisting on going around the room and clinking glasses with everyone.

The noise was so great that Becca woke, and she usually sleeps undisturbed. Mrs. Paddock and Mrs. Dill played with her nearly the whole night, so that was one less thing I had to be concerned about.

It was the first time I saw Mr. Wilson all week. He was away again, although no one knows where, not even Mrs. Thompson. Henry thinks he went to Lexington for a secret meeting.

Mr. Wilson didn't say anything special to me. Just treated me the same as usual. I think he did that so no one would know that we work together now.

I tried not to look at Molly, which is difficult even under ordinary circumstances. I had so little time that even if I wanted to look I dared not. Once, while Mr. Monk was playing with Mrs. Thompson, I saw her standing near the barroom. She turned away when she realized I was looking at her.

Telling People What's Right and What's Wrong

Henry is reading *Robinson Crusoe* now. He reads more books in a week than most read in a year. Sometimes he stays up all night. When Henry is doing something, he concentrates real hard. Like when he teaches the Armstrong boys, or helps Mr. Armstrong get the paper ready for Monday.

He tells me all the things he's learning from Mr. Armstrong. They're like two peas in a pod. They even have the same pear shape—that's what Mr. Wilson says, although he always says it with a laugh and never when either of them is around.

According to Henry, Mr. Armstrong learned everything he knows from reading and Henry says that's how he's going to educate himself.

I asked Henry what he would like to do when his service to Mr. Armstrong is up. He said he would like to buy lots of land so he could live in peace. Henry likes books more than he likes people, although there are exceptions—Mr. and Mrs. Armstrong, for instance. There isn't anything Henry wouldn't do for them. And me. I'll tell you this, if Henry Moody likes you there isn't a more steadfast friend to be found. But, in general, he prefers to keep to himself. Maybe that's why we're such good friends—because we're so different.

I'm not like Henry.

I'm not sure what I want to do but I am resolved to live in a busy place like Boston. I like living where there's plenty of people around all the time and there's always something to do.

I think if I had to say right now, I'd say I'd wish to be like Mr. Wilson and spend my days writing about important things and telling people what's right and what's wrong.

The talk with Henry got me to thinking. I saw Mr. Wilson later and asked if he had advice for someone who wanted to be a fine writer like him, and he said that the most important thing to remember is to never use two words when one will do. I can't wait till I am no longer a boy and can write like Mr. Wilson. The faster the better.

Red Ants and Walnuts

I helped Mrs. Thompson peel some apples Monday for a pie, and then we discovered that there was no more butter so I had to run to Mrs. Paddock's. Mrs. Thompson said to be sure Mrs. Paddock writes it down so we can repay her when we can.

I asked her about the red ants.

We have red ants now, which we can thank Queen George for.

King George has provided us with a plague of red coats and now Queen George has given us red ants—for it's her food they have come in search of.

They are all over the kitchen and it is impossible to get rid of them.

Mrs. Paddock told me I should try pouring boiling water on them, which I have, to little effect. I advised her of this and she said she wasn't surprised since they are quite combative.

Her next recommendation was brushing mercurous chloride where I see them coming and going. If that fails, she said, I should put walnuts in the closet.

I couldn't imagine why a plate of walnuts would help me, as I did not recognize walnuts as possessing any poisonous qualities, but Mrs. Paddock explained that red ants just can't resist walnuts. According to her, it's their favorite food. "So," she said, "as soon as they all climb up on the plate, just pick it up and fling them into the fire and that will be the end of that."

Mr. Wilson looks tired. His face has grown thin in recent weeks and his cheeks look hollow. He dresses with even less care than usual. He eats little and sleeps hardly at all. Lately he has been having his dinner in his tiny room, and when I come for it, it is still where I left it, untouched.

At night I can hear him walking around. He's always scribbling away with his quill flying across the pages. If I stand quietly outside his door, I can hear the unceasing scratching of his pen. In the mornings he asks for more candles. No matter how many I give him, it isn't enough.

He writes by moonlight if the moon is full. I am usually the first to arise, but now, when I get up to begin the day's chores, I find him already in the barroom working by the window, sitting in Mrs. Paddock's chair. He says he wants to catch the early-morning light. He says he has much work to do and time is running short. He says he must work when there is light.

Becca has a fever and Mrs. Thompson is most worried, as we all are. It has come upon her suddenly. One day she was her laughing, jolly self and now she just lies there. Even

Queen George's face-licking fails to provoke the usual giggles.

I think it would be better if we didn't dip her in the tub of cold water every morning.

Everyone fears smallpox, although no red spots have appeared as yet.

Dr. Endicott's little girl, Susan, was stricken with smallpox and Mrs. Thompson says she had to spend the past year in bed recovering.

The mail came and I brought Mr. Wilson's up to his room and divided the rest for those who will come by later.

There was a letter for Mrs. Dill. When she came in, I gave it to her and she asked me to read it to her. It was from her sister who lives in Braintree and told of a great tragedy. One of Mrs. Dill's sister's children came too close to the fire and her clothing went up in flames and she was badly burnt. She is not expected to last.

Mrs. Dill left the tavern in a state of great distress and Mrs. Paddock went with her.

Since we are coming to the end of the year, Mr. Wilson wants me to make sure all the accounts are properly posted by January 1.

I went over everything with Mrs. Thompson. I like to keep her current.

She was surprised that I take care of it all by myself now.

She asked if Mr. Wilson helped me and I told her he doesn't even look at it anymore, which is the truth. I think she was proud of me, but it's hard to tell because Mrs. Thompson doesn't like anyone to see what she's thinking.

She asked where I learned to figure so well. I told her that Mama taught me to add and subtract by the time I was four and multiply and divide by the time I was five. She said she thought that was a great benefit to me.

Becca is still poorly. Thankfully there is no vomiting or diarrhea. We have not seen any pocks on Becca's face and her fever has subsided. I gave her some pudding and cream and she ate it all up.

There are rumors of a smallpox epidemic breaking out in the British barracks. Some say they are secretly burying their dead at night so no one will be the wiser. Nobody knows for certain.

Jimmy Carr, Mr. Williams's apprentice, has run off. Mr. Williams placed a notice in the paper, hoping that he will be returned.

N O T I C E

JAMES CARR, my apprentice, has run off
this day. He is quite TALL and SLIM, with a
large head and black curly hair.

He is about nineteen years of age and
sometimes calls himself JAMES SMITH or
JIMMY SMITH.

He is an IRISH lad but speaks middling
English. He was wearing a blue cap, dirty
trousers, a checked shirt, a vest, half-worn
shoes and light-colored breeches.

A REWARD is offered to whoever secures said
apprentice and returns him to me.

Jonathan Williams

A True Patriot

Last night I went to the burying grounds at Copp's Hill. The place where Henry got bit by that snake. I hadn't been back there since that night.

I asked Henry if he wanted to go with me but he said he had to set some type for Mr. Armstrong. I think that was just an excuse and told him so. But he wouldn't budge, so I went alone.

I'm not quite sure why I went. Sometimes I just like to be scared. To see if I can take it. I don't like to be afraid of anything.

I didn't stay long, though. Not because I was scared but because I was cold.

On the way back, I saw that little Negro chimney sweep lurking about. His behavior was most suspicious, so I decided to follow him. I followed him for a few streets and then he stopped and began walking up and down, looking around as if he were expecting someone. I had to wait a long time and I was about to give up and head back to the tavern when I heard someone riding toward us, so I pulled back into the shadows. I couldn't see who the man was, even when he dismounted, but just as soon as he did, the sweep ran up to him and started speaking excitedly and pointing down the street. They walked in the direction the sweep was pointing and I followed, keeping as far back as I dared, fearing I would lose them if I didn't stay close. They stopped when they got to the entrance of a boarded-up warehouse.

The man gave the sweep something—a coin, I think—and knocked. The door was opened immediately—whoever was inside had been waiting impatiently for this man.

I couldn't see who opened the door, but when he stepped out of the doorway to pull the other man inside, I realized that he used his left arm because he had no right arm.

It was Mr. Palmer.

What was Mr. Palmer doing in a warehouse on Fish Street in the North End? Who was the man who came to see him? I wanted to leave right then and go back to the tavern and tell Mr. Wilson everything, but I thought it would be best if I stayed and tried to see what I could see.

Mr. Palmer looked quickly up and down Fish Street to see if he had been observed and, believing he was safe, closed the door.

I approached the warehouse and looked for a place where I might see what was going on inside. There was an opening where a board was missing but it was too high up. I climbed on top of a rain barrel that was standing next to the wall.

There they were, Mr. Palmer and the man who had come on horseback. There was no mistaking Mr. Palmer, even though I couldn't see anyone's face clearly. His right arm gave him away.

The two of them were leaning over a table looking at a piece of paper. It looked like the man was lecturing Mr. Palmer. He kept pointing a finger at Mr. Palmer and picking up the paper and showing it to him. It looked like he was pointing to particular words, but I couldn't see which ones.

The other man was moving like he was agitated and losing his patience rapidly. Suddenly, without any warning, he stormed out of the room and Mr. Palmer hurried after him.

I didn't know what to do. There was no time. I stood stock-still—not even breathing. I could hear them shouting at each other after they emerged from the warehouse, and then there was silence until I heard the other man gallop off, his horse's hooves clattering in the stillness of the night.

I waited, wanting to be sure that Mr. Palmer was gone, too.

When I was convinced it was safe, and not a moment before, I prepared to jump off the rain barrel and got the fright of my life. The little Negro sweep was standing there, waiting.

I didn't know what would happen next and was too afraid to move. Much to my astonishment the sweep reached up to help me down. I grabbed his hand and jumped to the ground. But that wasn't all. The sweep had, in the same motion, handed me a folded piece of paper. Immediately I knew it was the one the man had shown to Mr. Palmer.

"How did you get this?" I asked, my voice louder than I had intended.

The sweep stood there, motionless and mute, as if to say

getting it was enough, talking about it too dangerous. He looked at me with those sad eyes. It was like he was waiting to see if I was paying close attention. "Five," he whispered, and was gone before I could say, "Five what?"

When I got back to the tavern, I could see by the candlelight under the door that Mr. Wilson was still awake. I knocked but heard nothing. I knocked again and this time heard a gruff, "Enter."

Mr. Wilson's head was lost in a cloud of smoke, his pipe clenched tightly in his teeth and an empty ale tankard by his side.

He turned toward me and put down his quill. I knew I had better be brief. Mr. Wilson is always saying, "Be brief, Will, be brief."

I was brief, so brief that Mr. Wilson made me repeat everything. He wanted to know what the other man looked like, exactly where the warehouse was, and if I was certain it was Mr. Palmer in that room.

"Yes, sir," I replied without hesitation, both of us knowing it could be no other. There wasn't a man or woman in Boston Mr. Wilson didn't know and Mr. Palmer was the only one without a right arm.

Then, abruptly, Mr. Wilson turned his attention to the paper the sweep gave me.

June 8, 1774

Mr. Robert Palmer
71 Tremont Street
Boston, The Massachusette Bay Colony

Dear Mr. Palmer:

We are writing to you because the payment that must be forthcoming before we provide any goods is missing. The invoice numbers and receivers' names are also contractually necessary.

Of course it will be the primary goal and sole principal aim of our Mr. Leaders — who I have told of your problems — to alleviate the obstacles and satisfy any opposition to your plans.

Respectfully yours,

Jonathan Frost

President

81

He kept mumbling to himself, "Five, five, five," over and over. He stared down at the paper for the longest time, as if it would reveal something to him if only he looked long enough and hard enough. I had never seen him like this. I was afraid to move or make a sound.

He took up his quill and began to circle certain words. Then he went back to staring at it.

I couldn't imagine what he was doing. By now I had read what was written. It was simply a boring business letter from a man in London named Frost.

"That's it," Mr. Wilson said, sitting back at last, his blue eyes twinkling in the fading candlelight.

Then I saw what Mr. Wilson saw. It was not a business letter at all. Now that Mr. Wilson had circled every fifth word the real message, hidden within, was clear.

June 8, 1774

Mr. Robert Palmer
71 Tremont Street
Boston, The Massachusette Bay Colony

Dear Mr. Palmer:

We are writing to you because the payment that must be forthcoming before we provide any goods is missing. The invoice numbers and receivers' names are also contractually necessary.

Of course it will be the primary goal and sole principal aim of our Mr. Leaders — who I have told of your problems — to alleviate the obstacles and satisfy any opposition to your plans.

Respectfully yours,

Jonathan Frost

President

83

It was a coded message from a British agent to a spy—Mr. Palmer.

"Good work, Will," Mr. Wilson said, lighting his pipe. "You are an observant lad and a true patriot."

Winter 1774-75

MRS. THOMPSON'S IDLE HANDS
MR. WILSON HAS A CLOSE SHAVE
WELCOME TO THE WORLD
WHAT MOLLY DAVIS IS READING

Mrs. Thompson's Idle Hands

Mrs. Thompson knitted a pair of woolen mittens and a muffler for my birthday. I was so surprised—not only because she remembered it was my birthday, but because she has been knitting every morning for a month now and every time I asked her what she was knitting, she would say, "Just trying to keep my hands from being idle," which, frankly, didn't make much sense, since no one would ever accuse Mrs. Thompson of having idle hands, but I figured that was her way of telling me it wasn't any of my business.

I just said, Thank you, ma'am, but I had more to say than that, I just couldn't get it out.

Samuel Robbins fell through the ice and drowned. He was only eight. The weather is so warm that Frog Pond had not even frozen over completely.

Mr. Wilson Has a Close Shave

Mrs. Thompson reminded me to bank the fire carefully at night: raking up all the coals and covering them with the ashes so that in the morning I will be able to rekindle the flames without any trouble. If the embers die out overnight, it will be cold in the kitchen in the morning.

Mr. Wilson prefers to do his writing in the kitchen on cold days so he can be near the warmth and light of the fire. I don't blame him. The kitchen is the most comfortable room in the tavern.

He has been so busy lately. He hardly has time to see to it that he makes a neat appearance. Most of the time his rumpled clothes aren't even properly arranged. When he goes out, he just throws his tattered gray cloak over his shoulder and jams his hat even tighter.

Mrs. Thompson is always reminding him about this or that and Mr. Wilson just says, "I don't have time for that now, Elizabeth."

That's Mrs. Thompson's name, Elizabeth. Mr. Wilson's is John.

She really put her foot down yesterday. She ordered him to get a shave and a trim. Mr. Wilson does not powder his hair or wear a wig. He's a plain and sober man. She even insisted that I go with him to make sure he got there and didn't "go off on some little adventure."

After his haircut Mr. Davis left the steaming towel on Mr. Wilson's face while he sharpened his razor.

I watched him. I can't wait till I can shave. Mr. Wilson said he didn't think it would be long now.

On the way home Mr. Wilson said it was a clean, close shave and that he felt refreshed.

He also said, "There aren't many like Mrs. Thompson, Will, not many at all. We're two lucky lads, don't you think?"

I told him I did.

On the way back from Mr. Davis's we saw the most elegant four-wheeled coach I have ever seen. It must have been Mr. Dudley's because Henry told me he is one of the richest men in Boston. The coach had a leather top, polished silver mountings and a newly varnished harness, and it was drawn by six white horses. I realized it was the same coach that almost ran me down when I first came to town. I couldn't see Mr. Dudley himself and Mr. Wilson had already pulled his hat farther down his head and quickened his pace.

When I caught up, I said, "That was Mr. Dudley. Henry said he's the richest merchant in Boston," and Mr. Wilson said, "He's not a merchant, Will, he's just a thief like all the rest."

Mr. Wilson was working late and Mrs. Thompson said I should bring some ale up to his room.

He was cutting papers into long strips with a scissors. The strips lay curled up all over the floor covering the tops of his shoes like the freshly fallen snow outside. He said he didn't want to take the time to go down to the kitchen to burn the papers in the fire and didn't want them falling into the wrong hands.

Welcome to the World

Mrs. Thompson says I should try and keep Becca in the kitchen now that winter is upon us. This is not as easy as it might sound.

Becca is getting bigger every day, not as rapidly as Queen George and not as big, but she is growing and getting to know what she likes and what she doesn't like. She doesn't like being in her high chair anymore. Thinks she's too old for that. She likes being in the kitchen, but only for a while—then she gets bored and knows everyone's in the barroom and wants to go in there.

Mr. Monk is her favorite. Mr. Monk is Queen George's favorite, too. If she's missing, I know where to go to find her.

Last week Queen George came trotting home, looking as innocent as a newborn calf. She had a note pinned to her collar. It was from Mr. Monk and it said: *Don't bother fixing supper, dined with Mr. Monk, QG.*

We found out later that she was not exactly invited but had gotten up when no one was looking and taken Mr. Monk's supper somewhere and eaten it all herself.

I told Mrs. Thompson that maybe we should make Queen

George a turnspit dog. She didn't even know what a turnspit dog was so I had to explain. We would have Mr. Monk contrive a wheel that was big enough and wide enough for Queen George to walk in. A hot coal would be placed at her feet so that if she stopped walking she would get burnt and the contraption would be attached to a spit that would turn and cook the roast while Queen George walked the wheel.

Mrs. Thompson said I should be ashamed of myself for thinking thoughts like that, and besides, she said, where would we get a roast?

This morning I found Becca hiding behind the pantry playing with something she didn't want me to see. I was finally able to coax her out and make her show me. It was a pincushion that Mrs. Thompson said Mrs. Dill made for Becca when she was first born. I discovered it before she was able to do any harm and took it away so I could take out the pins. But Becca is an impatient lass and she hollered like a savage until I returned it to her.

The pincushion says: *Welcome to the World, Rebecca Thompson, July 4, 1772.*

Mr. Monk brought some chestnuts and we roasted them in a long-handled skillet in the fire. They tasted mighty good. I don't think Becca liked hers, because she spit most of it on the floor.

I have been feeling weak and achy because of the fever that does not seem to want to leave me. Mrs. Thompson gives me brandy and hot water before I go to sleep and brings down the footstove, which provides welcome extra warmth.

If having British soldiers camping right in the middle of town wasn't enough, they are now being put up in people's homes. There are three staying with Mr. and Mrs. Bacon, where there is little enough room.

What Molly Davis Is Reading

Henry said Molly Davis came into the shop yesterday. I haven't seen her since the night Mr. Monk brought his fiddle into the tavern.

She reads a lot, too, just like Henry. They both have a bookish inclination. Henry likes to read more than anything else in the world. It's no wonder that his spectacles are so thick. Sometimes, he tells me, he stays up most of the night reading.

Henry said Molly bought *Clarissa* and some drawing paper. He's going to read *Clarissa*, too, so he can have something to talk to her about the next time she comes in.

Mr. Armstrong said he could take one of the copies from the lending library. Mr. Armstrong told Henry that it was "admirable" that he wanted to read a book such as *Clarissa*.

Henry didn't tell Mr. Armstrong he wanted to read *Clarissa* just so he could talk to Molly Davis.

My fever is gone, thanks to Mrs. Thompson's care.

Henry asked me why I have been acting so odd lately. I think he suspects something, but I am sworn to secrecy. I dislike deceiving Henry. I know he can be trusted, but orders are orders.

TIME
FALSE FRIEND

Time

When Mr. Armstrong brought the newspaper this morning, everyone gathered around while he read Mr. Wilson's article aloud. I watched Mr. Palmer to see if I could detect anything odd in his behavior, but he just sat there listening like the others.

T I M E

It's TIME, brave *sons* of AMERICA.

Time to put aside our petty differences; postpone our individual agendas; cease cowering before our oppressors and begin our *glorious* march toward the *future*.

Time to enjoy the LIBERTY that is bestowed upon us by heaven.

It's TIME, brave *sons* of AMERICA.

Time for the KING to wake up; his PARLIAMENT to *face* up; their soldiers to pack up.

It's TIME, brave *sons* of AMERICA.

Time for the mother country to realize her children have grown; that they've chosen *freedom* over tyranny and liberty over oppression.

It's TIME, brave *sons* of AMERICA.

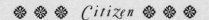

❀ ❀ ❀ *Citizen* ❀ ❀ ❀

All agreed Mr. Wilson wields a powerful pen. He chooses his words with great care and seems to pierce right through to the heart of the matter.

False Friend

Mr. Wilson has another assignment for me.

This one is more perilous, he said, pausing to see if I wanted to say anything. I told him I could look after myself.

He took me into the back room and took a panel off the wall, revealing a snug space hidden behind. It was just big enough for a boy my size. Mr. Wilson asked me to see if I could fit in there. I could—it was as if it were built just for me.

"Good, good," Mr. Wilson muttered to himself, and then, without hesitating, began explaining his plan to me.

"Tomorrow morning there will be a special meeting of the Committee. The usual gentlemen will be in attendance. I will begin by announcing that I have received the militia plans for the defense of the colony and wish to advise everyone of the present military circumstances. While I am speaking, I will be holding a paper conspicuously in my hand.

"At that point Mrs. Thompson will burst into the room, exhibiting great agitation. She will announce that there is a fire on Water Street.

"Everyone, of course, will immediately leave in order to lend a hand, myself included. I will leave the paper on the table.

"If Mr. Palmer is the false friend we think he is, he will not be able to resist taking that piece of paper. Somehow he will manage to remain behind, grab the paper and leave, hoping to appear to be joining the rest of us to fight the fire, but he won't be. He will be taking the paper somewhere and showing it to someone. I want to know who that someone is, Will. Do you understand?"

"You mean you want me to hide in there, sir?" I asked. Mr. Wilson said he wanted me to hide in there and keep watch through a tiny pinhole.

"As soon as our friend picks up the paper and leaves, I want you to follow him wherever he goes. You mustn't lose him, Will. No matter where he goes, you must follow him. It is of the utmost importance that we know where he goes with that paper and to whom he gives it. Do you understand, Will?"

I told him I did.

I don't think I slept at all, for in the morning I was up before first light, waiting in the back room. As soon as I heard someone enter the tavern, I crawled into the space and closed the panel tight before me.

There was no light other than the tiny beam coming through the pinhole, and just as little air. I hoped I didn't have to stay there too long, because the longer I was in there, the more afraid I was that I would sneeze or cough and give the whole thing away.

I was getting sleepy because it was so dark and quiet, and then I heard voices. Mr. Monk, Dr. Endicott, Mr. Cummings, and Mr. Palmer.

Mr. Wilson hurried everyone along, saying that he had a confidential announcement.

I could see Mr. Palmer through the pinhole. He was standing at the back of the room, next to Dr. Endicott.

Mrs. Thompson rushed in right on schedule and made her announcement. I must say she was quite convincing, and everyone followed her out, including Mr. Palmer, who had not stayed behind as Mr. Wilson had predicted.

Maybe we were wrong about him, I thought. Maybe the meeting in the warehouse with that man just looked suspicious. Everything looks suspicious these days. Maybe there was really nothing to it.

I was about to punch open the panel and leave when Mr. Palmer reappeared. He backed in, keeping an eye out to see if anyone in the barroom was watching him. Once he was in, he wheeled around and surveyed the room, making sure he was alone—for a moment I was certain his eyes were looking right through the pinhole directly into mine and that he knew I was there, hidden behind the wall, spying on him. But then his eyes shifted to the table and he snatched up the paper with his one hand and stuffed it into his pocket and, after glancing once more around the room, was gone.

I was so stunned that all this was happening just as Mr. Wilson said it would that I almost forgot my mission. I kicked out the panel and ran through the barroom and out the side door just in time to see Mr. Palmer disappear down Cornhill, past Water, where the fire was supposed to be, and turn down Milk Street. There was no doubt where he was heading. He was going down Milk Street to the wharf. I took a cutoff down Tanner's Lane to Hutchinson and followed him to Griffin's Wharf.

I got there just in time to see him being helped down into a long boat, which was then rowed out into the harbor by British sailors.

I was going to lose him if I just stood there. I couldn't follow him. I could swim, but the water would be too cold. I wouldn't last. Soon I would lose sight of him. He would be too far out in the harbor. Then I had a thought. Mr. Williams's shop on Cow Lane. Cow Lane wasn't far from Griffin's Wharf. Maybe I could make it there and back in time.

I had to hope he would understand. I had to hope I could trust him.

I was out of breath when I got there but couldn't spare any time.

"I need this" was all I could manage. Mrs. Williams looked astonished—fortunately she made no move to stop me. Mr. Williams must have been in the back, as usual, working. I ran all the way back, knowing I could rest once I got to the wharf.

I put the spyglass up to my eye, my heart pounding, fearful I had taken too long, scanning the water for his long boat.

There he was. I had gotten back just in time.

Mr. Palmer's long boat had pulled up alongside one of the

warships in the harbor. I held the spyglass firmly in place and watched his every move as he was helped up the sides of the enormous vessel.

Mr. Wilson made me go over everything that happened and urged me not to leave anything out. Just like the last time. When I finished, he asked me only one question, but I could tell by the look in his eye it was an important one.

"Did you see the name of the ship, Will?"

"I did, sir," I replied. "It was the *Viper*, sir."

Mr. Wilson nodded his head and said, "That's just where I thought he'd go. Just where I thought he'd go."

Chips for Kindling

Mrs. Thompson sent me to Mr. Monk's to get some chips for kindling.

I decided to take Becca and Queen George with me. I thought they would be good company, for it's a long walk, and it would be nice for Becca to be out in the snow. I bundled her up from head to foot.

Mr. Monk helped me pile the chips on the sled and offered to go back with us to the tavern. I told him we would be fine, which we were for a while.

Becca insisted on walking, which slowed us down since she doesn't walk that fast under the best of circumstances and the snow was nearly up to her waist. Queen George spent her time running circles around us and trying to catch snowflakes with great enthusiasm and little result. The confused look she wore, wondering where they had gone to when she had them right in her sights, made Becca and me laugh. But our laughter wasn't the only sound I heard.

A burly British soldier, singing in a loud voice and half out of his wits, it appeared to me, was coming toward us.

He grabbed me rudely by the arm and ordered me to "halt and reveal what treasure lay hidden under that blanket—muskets for your friends, no doubt," he said.

I told him they were only chips for kindling, but he said, "Let's see," pushed me out of the way and yanked off the blanket. He stared at the pile of chips as if they were the last things in the world he expected to see there.

I took advantage of his bewilderment and picked up Becca, who could tell something was wrong and let me hold her.

Queen George was not so cooperative. She watched the soldier warily and growled low and slow.

She does not like lobsterbacks any more than we do and when one passes by the tavern she heads for the door and sniffs and scratches furiously with her front paws.

We have to keep a close eye on her. Last week Mr. Bacon's dog was killed by a soldier who claims that the dog was trained to attack redcoats on sight and was bearing his teeth at him in preparation. Just ran the poor beast through with a bayonet.

The soldier walked around the sled, eyeing the pile of chips suspiciously and muttering something to himself. I could see the muscles of his jaw twitching and I could smell that he was bold with liquor.

"It must have taken a long time to pile all those chips on that sled," he said.

"Yes, sir, it did," I replied as courteously as I could, hoping that would put an end to our conversation. But he started walking around the sled again, muttering to himself all the while, his hands clasped behind his back.

Queen George was up now and so was the hair on the top of her head. I feared she was about to do something. So did the soldier, who was watching her when he wasn't looking at the sled. I pushed her away with my leg but she returned at once like a big ball on the end of a band.

It was cold and I was starting to shiver. Becca was burrowing into my chest. I wished he'd move on so we could all go home. Then, with no warning, he kicked the sled over with his heavy boot, scattering all the chips into the deep snow.

"Looks like you won't be getting home for quite a while, doesn't it, boy?" He laughed and went walking down the street singing in that same loud voice.

I didn't bother with the chips and put Becca on the sled, holding on to Queen George's ample neck so she wouldn't go after the soldier.

We were all tired and cold when we got back to the tavern.

Innocent citizens can hardly walk down the street without being confronted by them. They jab you in the ribs with the butts of their bayonets and then laugh like they've heard the best joke. They utter abuse and threats for no reason, causing an uproar wherever they go. They're as thick as bees.

Last week Mr. Davenport, the butcher, was tripped by one of them while carrying something and found himself lying in the mud. The soldiers stood around pointing and ridiculing

Mr. Davenport. They stopped when the other butchers in the market came out of their stalls, wiping their hands on their aprons and circling round the soldiers, sharpened cleavers and knives at the ready.

Mr. Davenport said he thought for certain blood would be running with the mud in no time, but a British officer stepped in the middle of the circle and ordered the soldier who tripped Mr. Davenport back to his barracks, thereby restoring order.

But this single gesture is cold comfort compared to the terror that follows in their wake day after day.

Many of the Negro slaves in town are angry now because the soldiers have told them that when they take over they will be rewarded with their freedom. They encourage the Negros to slit their masters' throats, thereby hastening that day.

That's how it is now.

Mr. Wilson says it will not be long before something sparks the fuse that will cause our world to explode into a thousand pieces.

Dr. Endicott's Son

Dr. Endicott has asked his son to leave the house. There was silence Tuesday night following this announcement, everyone realizing that a terrible personal ordeal was taking place.

He said the decision broke his heart, but he saw no other choice in light of his son's continued loyalty to the Crown and the recent letter in the paper. It was unknown at first who wrote it, since it was signed *A True and Faithful Subject of His Majesty*, but everyone was talking about it and trying to guess the author.

Dr. Endicott was sent an anonymous note informing him that the person who penned such poison was none other than his own son. Dr. Endicott confronted him with this disturbing accusation and he not only admitted writing the letter but said he was proud of it. No one spoke except for Mr. Palmer, who went on at some length, ending with the suggestion that the king was a fool and like all fools he should have his head cut off. You could tell he was real nervous because he was stuttering even more than usual.

My Fellow British Subjects,

Proper subordination to the supreme authority of the British Empire is what is called for. The King deserves nothing less than our loyalty and obedience. His Parliament nothing less than our respect and admiration.

This is how it has always been and how it should continue to be. Pay no heed to the ravings of a small group of rebellious, blaspheming schemers, few in number and of the lowest kind, who suggest we throw off the rule of a great and good king who has done much for us in the past and will continue to do so in future. We must only have the good sense to refrain from encouraging these boorish adventurers who are responsible for the current lamentable state of affairs, where contempt for authority and an unwillingness to submit to the rule of the law is looked upon with approval.

All loose talk of freedom and outrageous claims of natural rights by these wicked, unruly colonists—all bankrupt in reputation—is sheer folly. They are put forth by an irresponsible local faction interested only in lining their own pockets at the expense of all who are blind and deluded enough to follow them.

Do not be fooled by these New England fanatics, who have been ungovernable since the start. They are traitors and hypocrites, leading you down the road to mob rule, anarchy and worse.

Separation from the mother country can only prove to be a painful descent into darkness, a darkness from which we will never return.

Reconciliation is the route we must follow— not separation.

A True and Faithful Subject of His Majesty

Dr. Endicott's son has decided to pack up and sail for England. He does not plan to return.

No One Has Seen Henry's Spectacles

One of the lobsterbacks caught Henry Moody.

He was watching them march down King Street and was standing in a crowd of bully boys from the North End who were yelling and pelting them with snowballs packed with gravel, icicles that hung from the eaves and chunks of ice from the street. Some of the soldiers tried to slap the snowballs away with shovels but one of the boys from the North End hit a lobsterback in the cheek and cut him so badly he fell to the ice.

The bully boys weren't afraid of the soldiers because they knew they were under strict orders not to fire back, even in self-defense. But the soldiers charged the crowd and they all ran, and Henry had no choice but to run with them—he knew the soldiers would never sit still long enough for him to explain that he wasn't with them or that he hadn't thrown anything.

Henry gave them a good run for a time but he couldn't run very fast and couldn't run very long, fat as he is.

One of the soldiers finally trapped him on Mackrell Lane. He struck Henry on the side of his head with the buttend of his bayonet. Henry was dazed and tried to run but there was nowhere to go. The soldier followed him down the alley and hit him again and again until his face was a bloody pulp and he was no longer moving.

Mrs. Thompson says he is hurt very badly.

I went to see Henry Moody today. Mr. Armstrong told Mr. Wilson that the time was short.

When I got there Mrs. Armstrong said that Henry was upstairs sleeping, but that I should go up. He was in the bed with the covers covering everything but his eyes and the top of his head. There were even bruises on the top of his head. He looked tired and scared. He didn't know who I was at first, even though he was awake and his eyes were open, because he didn't have his spectacles on. Henry can't see anything without his spectacles.

"Henry," I said, although I wasn't sure he heard me. "It's me, Will." He narrowed his eyes, trying to make out who I was.

"Where are your spectacles?" I asked, but he didn't answer. It was too much, watching him lie there, enduring this pain and unable to see on top of it all. I had to find his spectacles.

I left without a word of explanation to either Mr. Armstrong, who was sitting in the corner of the room, or to Mrs. Armstrong, who remained downstairs keeping an eye on the shop.

They weren't on Mackrell Lane, where they found Henry. They were just around the corner, on King Street. That meant he couldn't see the face of the soldier who had done this to him.

One of the lenses was cracked, but it was a clean crack and would do just fine.

He was sleeping when I got back, so I decided not to wake him. I just sat there with Mr. Armstrong, who had a book in his lap but wasn't reading it. I wanted to say something to him but remained silent.

Henry coughed and woke himself up with a start, as if struggling to escape from some horrible dream.

"Henry," I said, "I found your spectacles."

He turned in my direction but that was all. He didn't say a word.

I went over to the bed and put the spectacles on his swollen face.

He seemed to want me to come nearer, so I leaned over. He tried to speak but his lips were parched and cracked and he had little strength left. His lips moved, but no sound came forth.

Then I could hear the faintest whisper.

"Will," he said, "my good and true friend."

But that was all. It looked like he had gone back to sleep.

I turned to Mr. Armstrong and he motioned for me to leave and wait downstairs.

A few minutes later he came down and told me and Mrs. Armstrong that poor Henry had departed this earth.

Spring 1775

In Cold Blood

Henry Moody was buried today.

His coffin was carried on a sled to the burying grounds on Copp's Hill—the same one where we first became friends. The runners made an eerie sound on the hard-packed snow. Mrs. Armstrong was unable to attend, caring for the two boys, who miss their tutor dearly, and overcome herself with grief. Mr. Armstrong is in a state of utter despair. Everyone else was there, including Mr. Palmer.

The ground was too hard to dig a grave, and so Henry, in his wooden box, was laid on the ground until it thaws and he can be buried properly. Mr. Paddock etched the word *Patriot* on the box. Henry would have been proud of that. Mr. Wilson spoke. I have never heard him sound so sad.

"Now their hands are dripping with the blood of childish innocence."

That was all he said.

It was a terrible day.

Mr. Wilson has not left his room. He writes day and night, sleeping little. He barely touches the food I bring him and we are running low on candles. I am having great difficulty keeping him supplied with these as well as quills for his pen. This morning I mixed the powder and water to make more ink and brought it up with his pint of ale. This seemed to please him, although he did not stop writing, even for a moment.

I brought him a footstove filled with hot coals to help him keep warm and prevent his toes from getting numb. It is quite cold in his room.

Mr. Armstrong ran Mr. Wilson's article with a black border around it:

IN COLD BLOOD

*T*here was blood on the soft snow that cushioned the hard fall of HENRY MOODY.

NOW THERE IS BLOOD ON
THEIR BRUTISH BRITISH HANDS.

Let every father tell his children the story of HENRY MOODY so that generation unto generation no one will ever forget what happened here.

THERE CAN BE NO MORE HENRY MOODYS.

There can be no more talk of reconciliation and reunion. We must leave that to the town fool. Talk of reconciliation is the talk of the weak. The strong are ready to take up arms.

WE MUST STOP BEHAVING LIKE BOYS
AND START BEHAVING LIKE MEN.

*BLOOD HAS BEEN SHED AND FOR IT BLOOD
MUST ATONE.*

If violence is our only alternative, then let us not delay. Guided by our benevolent creator, let us see to it that righteousness and justice TRIUMPH over *TYRANNY* and *OPPRESSION*. Let us see to it that we do not rest until we have established a society where men can be free and equal.

The heartless BRITISH BUTCHERS must come to know that the next time *IT WILL BE THEIR BLOOD* that turns the snow crimson.

THEY MUST COME TO KNOW THAT OUR WILL IS AS HARD AND TRUE AS THE STEEL OF THE BAYONETS THEY CARRY.

They must come to know that they will PAY DEARLY for their TRESPASSES, for once the dogs of war are unleashed there will be precious little time for wishing it were otherwise.

THEY will be fighting far from home, having journeyed across a vast and hazardous ocean to a hostile land where they will find neither food nor friend, unwelcome for as long as they insist on spreading terror throughout our peaceful country and willfully harming our innocent children.

WE will be fighting in our own fields, fresh from our

own farms, defending our own homes, unlimited in number, standing one behind the other ready if and when one of us should fall, for we are as a band of brothers. Patriots fueled by the flame of freedom that burns within our very souls, and driven forward by the love of liberty that lights our path.

DO NOT UNDERESTIMATE THE FIRMNESS OF OUR RESOLVE.

The others will stand with us, for they know we are engaged in a glorious struggle.

VIRGINIANS, NEW ENGLANDERS, PENNSYLVANIANS, MARYLANDERS.

NO, I SAY.

AMERICANS.

AMERICANS one and all.

And as AMERICANS, we are prepared to die for our country.

We shall be INDEPENDENT. Nothing short of that will suffice or satisfy.

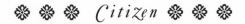

❖ ❖ ❖ *Citizen* ❖ ❖ ❖

Three Little Girls

Yesterday Mrs. Nelson's three little girls lost their lives due to a most unfortunate accident. Mrs. Nelson ordered some medicine from Mr. Clapham, the apothecary, and the wrong medicine was sent by mistake. No one knows yet where the fault lies.

The three little girls were suffering severely from the throat distemper that has plagued the town recently. Dr. Endicott tried bleeding them but that did nothing to relieve their pain and discomfort, which continued as before. It was the hope that the medicine would provide the answer.

The medicine was administered to the three unfortunate children as soon as it arrived. Much to everyone's shock all three went into violent convulsions immediately and died within hours. Dr. Endicott was sent for but there was nothing he could do.

Mrs. Nelson is terribly melancholy and Mrs. Thompson is with her.

FIRE BELLS
WAR IS JUST AROUND THE CORNER
SENDING A BOY TO DO A MAN'S JOB
CHAOS REIGNS

Fire Bells

There was a dreadful fire last night near Copp's Hill. Fire bells rang out through the night. The small wooden houses are so closely crowded together that nearly every one was burned to the ground, even though the firemen arrived on the scene with their pumping engines and worked with great haste.

It was only thanks to their valiant efforts that some of the houses were saved and the fire was prevented from spreading to other parts of town. They used their axes and hooks to tear down dwellings that were already burnt beyond saving in order to save others not yet touched, but in the fire's path.

Their work was made more difficult by the darkness of the moonless night.

Finally, by dawn, the blaze had died out, thankfully no wind blowing up to rekindle the embers.

Last week ten soldiers, all tied one to the other, were whipped on the Common. Their backs were bared despite the cold, and some, who could not take it, fell to the ground crying out and pleading for mercy.

Mr. Wilson asked me if I knew how to ride. At first I thought he was joking with me. I thought everyone knew how to ride. But as it turns out, Mr. Wilson has never had occasion to learn.

Now, he says, it would be best if he knew how—it might come in handy soon, was how he put it. He asked if I would give him a lesson or two. I agreed and Mr. Monk, who is busy night and day repairing firearms, is going to have Blue, his most surefooted mare, ready for us in the morning. Blue doesn't look blue—she's reddish brown—just that she always looks like she's feeling blue. That's why Mr. Monk calls her Blue.

War Is Just Around the Corner

There was a great deal of excitement at last night's meeting. The back room was even more crowded than usual because many patriots were in attendance from Concord, Lexington and even as far away as Worcester.

They report that there is great agitation in the countryside, where the people are in a constant state of alarm. They are determined to defend their rights and thousands from all over New England are seeing to it that their arms are in good working order: oiling the locks of their muskets, gathering their powder horns and pouches and melting lead for bullets.

They are prepared to march at a minute's warning. Many want to attack now and drive the British out of Boston once and for all.

British soldiers have been spotted in various locations outside of town wearing ill-fitting civilian clothes. Presumably they are in disguise so that they might pass unnoticed in order to gather information. Two were seen sketching the roads, drawing maps and noting the location of bridges. They seemed unaware of how conspicuous they were and that their every move is watched and reported on daily.

Mr. Monk thinks the British are preparing for something. The officers drill the men incessantly, parading them in rigid formations and putting them through endless inspections. Although the Committee knows they are preparing to march out of Boston, their exact destination is unknown.

"We are drawing closer to a conflict every day," Mr. Armstrong added. "New England is a powder keg. One spark and it will explode."

Mr. Cummings said that if the British make a move "they will be sorry they ever set foot on our sacred soil."

Then there was quiet, and I could almost imagine everyone looking at Mr. Wilson to see if he had anything to say.

"War is just around the corner," Mr. Wilson said.

More soldiers are arriving every day.

Mr. Wilson wants me to ride out to Roxbury tonight. He has received information that Mr. Palmer is secretly meeting an important British officer who has just arrived from England at Mr. Dudley's house.

Mr. Dudley is a man of capital and property. He has a grand house in Roxbury, although I have never seen it myself.

I reminded Mr. Wilson that it was Tuesday and Mr. Palmer would be at the Committee meeting tonight. But Mr. Wilson said that Mr. Palmer has sent word that he was confined to bed with a bad case of the gout and would be unable to attend tonight's meeting.

Mr. Wilson thinks that is precisely why Mr. Palmer's meeting is taking place on a Tuesday. That way, Mr. Wilson says, Mr. Palmer will feel safe, knowing that everyone will be at the tavern and therefore unlikely to see him and his companions in their nefarious activities.

"Observe everything you can, Will," Mr. Wilson said. "Who's there, who sits where and talks to whom. What they look like, the clothes they wear. The smallest detail might tell us more than you can imagine. But be sure to remain out of sight."

Mr. Monk had Blue all saddled up and ready to go. We set off at a smooth trot, slipping quietly past the sentries at the Neck. We encountered no difficulties, although the cold rain made the long ride uncomfortable. Thankfully there was no lightning.

It wasn't hard to find Mr. Dudley's house. It appeared right after I crossed the wobbly plank bridge, just as Mr. Wilson had said it would. I could see it even in the distance. There were so many candles lit, it looked like it was glowing in the forest. It was the grandest house I had ever seen.

I tied Blue to a tree and crouched down, content to just watch for a while before I moved closer.

When I was satisfied that it was safe, I moved closer to the house, thankful for the silence afforded by the muffling sound of the rain and the dampness of the ground. I stopped when I got to the carriage house, waiting a few minutes, and made my way to the gazebo before approaching the house. I could see everything through the big windows that everyone in town knows Mr. Dudley had specially made for him in England.

Mr. Palmer appeared to be already in his cups, talking excitedly to the British officer seated next to him. Mr. Palmer always likes to take two hours to tell you something that should take two minutes.

Mr. Dudley was dressed in fine fashion: red slippers, white silk stockings, black satin breeches and embroidered vest and an orange velvet coat. His well-known gold-tipped walking stick was leaning on his chair.

He sat at the head of the table carving an enormous roast and listening intently to the conversation between Mr.

Palmer and the British officer. Mr. Dudley cut his meat into little pieces with his knife, which he held in one hand while he speared the meat with the fork he held in the other. After each bite he carefully wiped his lips with a cloth. I have never seen anyone do that. Eat with a fork that way or use a cloth.

It was indeed an elegant dinner. Mr. Dudley's Negro servants darted in and out of the room bearing tray upon tray of food and making certain that the wineglasses were filled to the brim.

After everyone had eaten bounteously and the desserts—jellies, trifles and creams topped with almonds and raisins—had been served, Mr. Dudley ordered the servants out of the room with a wave of his hand.

He took a small gold snuffbox out from his vest pocket, opened the lid and took a pinch, which he placed in each nostril. Satisfied, he stood up and raised his wineglass, proposing, it appeared, to make a toast to Mr. Palmer, who smiled sheepishly like he was being congratulated on a job well done.

It was just then I heard something.

I started to turn and look in the direction the sound was coming from, but I stopped myself and froze, hoping whoever it was hadn't seen me and would pass by or, if I was lucky enough, it would turn out to be an animal sniffing around to see who the intruder was.

But then there was another sound. A step. It was no animal,

that was certain. It was too large, I could tell, and he was coming toward me.

I decided to run for it, and sure enough whoever it was immediately gave chase, at one point, before I pulled away, being only inches from my heels.

I ran through the woods as fast as I could, hoping to get back to Blue in time to make my escape. The low-hanging branches of the trees whipped my face, stinging me, and it got so bad I had to put up my arms to protect my face. The treacherously wet and slimy undergrowth concerned me so much that I didn't see the big, half-hidden tree root and tripped, flying head over heels and landing dazed but unhurt.

I forced myself to get up quickly but there he was, standing over me, laughing just like all the lobsterbacks.

"Leave it to these colonists, sending a boy to do a man's job," he said. "They're not a bunch of rebels, they're just a bunch of rabble." He liked his simple joke so much he started laughing all over again, and the more he thought about it, the funnier it got and the harder he laughed until he had to hold his big, fat stomach with both hands because he was afraid it was going to burst from all the merriment, and I thought I'd never have a better chance than this and so, in one swift motion, I pulled my knife out of my boot, and before the rascal realized what was happening to him, I slit his nostril nearly in two, straight up his nose, to his eyes, and half off his ugly British face.

The blood burst forth like an undammed river, gushing in such quantity that I thought for sure he would die right then and there, which would grieve me not one bit. He grabbed his face and screamed something at me that I was unable to decipher because his hands were clasped so firmly over his mouth, that alone making it hard to hear what he was saying. Also because there was so much blood spilling over his hands and seeping through his fingers, he sounded more like someone who was drowning than someone who was speaking.

You could see he was in a most distressed state.

I really wasn't interested in what he was saying anyway, and by now he had dropped to the ground, emitting the most hideous howls and kicking around foolishly, as if that would do him any good.

I leaned down and looked him right in the eyes. He was staring back at me like a poisoned pig. I spit in his face and said, "That's for Henry Moody," even though I knew he was too busy with what was bothering him to listen to me and wouldn't understand even if he weren't.

Blue was waiting patiently, good animal that she was, and I grabbed a fistful of her mane, spurred her over a low stone wall and we galloped back to Boston, which she seemed as happy to return to as me.

When I arrived back at the tavern, Mr. Wilson, seeing the state I was in, became quite agitated. I did not realize it, but

I was covered head to toe with the British soldier's blood, which Mr. Wilson thought was mine, and therefore that I was severely injured.

I assured him that I was in no way hurt and he was greatly relieved.

But even then he insisted that I first get out of my cold, wet clothes and cover myself with a blanket, which I must say did provide much relief.

I then proceeded to tell him everything I saw and everything that happened, including my harrowing encounter and narrow escape.

Mr. Wilson seemed especially interested in the British officer at Mr. Dudley's house. He wanted to know what he looked like and I told him: He was short, had a large head, flaming red hair, bushy eyebrows and big floppy ears and listened more than he spoke.

This information seemed to please Mr. Wilson.

Chaos Reigns

There are reports that there has been fighting between the British and the patriot militia on Lexington Common.

They say the British went out in search of cannons and powder stores and got more than they bargained for in return.

There are also reports of skirmishes near Concord Bridge. The British have suffered grave casualties and have been forced to retreat back to Boston. They have become like wild beasts and are retaliating by killing every living thing they come across—chickens, hogs, cattle—and by setting fire to the houses in their path, murdering all those within—women and children included.

Every carriage, chaise and coach is being used to carry the bloodied British soldiers back into town. It is a melancholy scene: The horrible sounds of their tortured screams are almost too much to bear. It has been like this for days. The town has been turned into a hospital as the wounded are tended to while the dead await burial.

All are agitated and eager for news, although wild tales are everywhere and rumors and inventions spread with alarming speed. The turmoil is unceasing.

Mr. Williams was arrested yesterday just for wiping his face with a handkerchief. The British say it was some kind of signal.

All talk is that war has come.

Those who can are leaving Boston to join the patriots, who control the countryside. They say it is no longer safe here now that British blood has been spilled.

Passes are being issued to anyone wishing to leave, although they must give up their firearms and weapons—knives included. They are to be deposited for safekeeping at Faneuil Hall with the owners' names, so that they can be reclaimed at the proper time.

While all this is happening, the loyalists from the country-side are flocking into town, seeking the safety of the British soldiers and warships in the harbor. They fear they are no longer safe in their own communities and will be murdered in their beds by their patriot neighbors.

People are loading up wagons and leaving as soon as they can. They pile bundles onto wagons and their bewildered children string along behind.

Chaos reigns.

Mr. and Mrs. Paddock have already departed for Hingham and have taken Mrs. Dill with them. Mr. Monk and Mr. Davis have gone to join up with the militia. Molly is already gone, her papa's knife sewn into the lining of her cloak. Mr. Davis sent her off with Dr. Endicott as soon as the wounded British troops began arriving back in town, returning from Lexington and Concord.

Mr. and Mrs. Armstrong and the boys are leaving tomorrow.

Mr. Wilson must leave soon, too. If he delays, the British will send him to England to stand trial or worse. He says he knows a place where we all can stay.

Mrs. Thompson refuses to leave.

She says she was born in Boston and has every intention of dying in Boston. "I can't pick up and leave, forsaking everything and heading for who knows where."

The tavern is all she has in the world and she says she can't just let the British do with it what they want.

She and Becca and Queen George can get on very well on

their own and we should all leave while we can, she said. There are rumors that the British are going to stop giving out the passes and then it will be too late to leave.

"I can take care of myself," she said.

Mr. Wilson turned to me. Although not one word passed between us, he knew.

I have decided to stay here with Mrs. Thompson.

Epilogue

Molly Davis and Colonel Matthew Chaney were married in February, 1783, the year the Revolutionary War ended. Chaney served with distinction throughout, helping train the newly formed Continental Army. He never returned to his native England.

Molly became well known for her colorful paintings, which decorated tin trays, teapots, clock faces and boxes. They had six children, all boys.

Mr. Armstrong, side by side with Mr. Davis, was killed by British soldiers during their assault on Breed's Hill in June 1775. Both men had run out of ammunition. This bloody encounter has since become known to history as the Battle of Bunker Hill.

Mrs. Armstrong and her sons returned to Boston after the war, where the two boys reestablished their father's printing and bookselling businesses, expanding both into successful financial enterprises.

Dr. Endicott served as a surgeon during the war. Mr. Monk was captured and died aboard a British prison ship. Mrs. Dill died in the fall of 1775 when a dysentery epidemic struck New England. Mrs. Paddock choked to death while eating her dinner one night. She died without being able to get up from her seat.

Will and Mrs. Thompson were forced, like many in Boston during the year-long occupation of that city, to rent rooms to British soldiers.

After the war Will's hard work and economic watchfulness, combined with Mrs. Thompson's gracious personality, resulted in the tavern's thriving and becoming a popular "watering hole." It became a particular favorite of Boston politicians.

Mrs. Thompson lived long enough to see Will marry her eighteen-year-old daughter Becca, who turned out to be an intelligent and independent girl. She became a teacher and taught for many years at School Street, accompanied by her dog, Queen George II.

Will and Becca had two children, one named Henry and the other Ben, after Mr. Wilson.

Mr. Wilson mysteriously disappeared after leaving Boston in the spring of 1775. Some say he went west, ending up in San Francisco. Others say he traveled down to New York City, where he found work writing for a small newspaper in Brooklyn. They point to the articles in the Brooklyn paper— mostly humorous sketches about local eccentrics that they say are unmistakably Wilson's writing. There is, however, no concrete evidence of his whereabouts.

After Mrs. Thompson died, Will discovered a letter that revealed how she and Mr. Wilson had come to know each other. The letter, apparently written the night before Mr. Wilson left Boston, thanked her for everything she had done for him. Mr. Wilson, it seems, had been married to Mrs. Thompson's older sister. When she died, along with the baby, in childbirth, the grief-stricken Mr. Wilson came to live at the Seven Stars Tavern.

Mrs. Thompson steadfastly refused to allow any soldier to stay in Mr. Wilson's room during the British occupation and miraculously, no one questioned her wishes.

There is no record of the Negro sweep's existence other than in Will's notes.

Mr. Palmer also remained in Boston—his traitorous activities known only to a handful. However, in the summer of 1778 he went for a ride and, it is believed, someone placed glass shards under his saddle. As a result he was thrown by his horse and seriously injured. He never recovered and died, painfully bedridden, a year later.

Life in America
in 1774

Historical Note

Many people assume that the American Revolution began in 1776 when the Declaration of Independence was signed, but the truth is much more complicated than that. In fact, it took many years for the Thirteen Colonies to decide to unite as one and seek their independence from England.

From the very beginning when the Pilgrims first landed at Plymouth Rock, the colonies had been under British rule. England enforced many regulations on property, imports and exports. The colonists cooperated because they needed to be able to sell their crops to other countries, and to buy supplies not produced in America like sugar, rice and tea.

In 1760, King George III took the British throne and became the ruler of the entire British Empire. With the assistance of the powerful British Parliament (which is similar to our Congress), King George III proclaimed new taxes and passed new laws that affected the colonies badly.

England and France were also bitter enemies. The two countries fought repeatedly for control of the ever-growing territory of what is now the United States and Canada. As the American colonies grew in population, they inevitably expanded geographically. As a result, the Native American peoples were pushed out of the land where they had lived for many generations, and England and France fought over everything else.

Finally, after what is known as the French and Indian War, a peace agreement called the Treaty of Paris was signed in 1763. This treaty gave England full control of Canada and the American colonies.

Those long years of war had been very expensive, and England wanted the colonists to pay for the privilege of having British troops defend them. England felt that a permanent force of British troops should be stationed in America, and that would cost a great deal of money. So King George III and Parliament promptly began imposing even more taxes. Because the colonists had no direct representation in Parliament, this was taxation without representation.

In 1764, England passed the Sugar Act, which added new, heavy fees to products such as sugar and wine. This was highly unpopular in America and led to protests and demonstrations. The Currency Act, instituted that same year, raised taxes on all American exports from two and a half percent to five percent of the total value.

Then, in 1765, the Stamp Act was created. Now the colonists had to pay extra duty, or customs, taxes on newspapers, legal documents and other necessary papers. Many colonists were upset about this, and what had once been peaceful protests now became violent riots. Pamphlets were published criticizing King George III and suggesting that it was time for the colonies to control their own destiny.

After a year of angry demonstrations, England finally repealed the Stamp Act. But in its place, the even more restrictive Townshend Acts of 1767 were imposed. These acts taxed crucial products such as paper, tea, glass, lead and painting supplies. The rebel colonists, who were now calling themselves "patriots," responded with still more protests and boycotts. However, the patriots were still a minority, and many colonists continued to support the throne. The patriots bitterly referred to those supporters as loyalists, or Tories.

The rebellion was at its strongest in the historically independent and feisty colony of Massachusetts. Recognizing this, England sent extra troops to occupy Massachusetts in 1768, which just raised tensions all the more. The British troops wore distinctive uniforms and were known as redcoats. Some colonists sarcastically called them lobsterbacks because they thought the bright red jackets resembled cooked lobsters.

In March 1770, an angry mob in Boston began throwing snowballs at a detachment of redcoats. The British soldiers responded to this rather minor attack by opening fire. Several civilians were killed, and this event became known as the Boston Massacre. The first man shot was Crispus Attucks. He is considered by many to be the first person killed in the Revolutionary War, even though actual combat was still years away.

With each new outrage, more colonists began to rebel. The movement toward independence was growing. In 1772, a

British schooner called the *Gaspee*, that was used to enforce revenue laws, hit a sandbar while patrolling the waters near Providence, Rhode Island. A group of patriots promptly boarded the ship and burned it.

Realizing that they were losing control, the British authorities tried to squash the rebellion. Unfortunately, their tactics only made the patriots more defiant. England passed the Tea Act of 1773, giving the East India Company a monopoly on selling tea. It may not have seemed important to King George and Parliament, but for many patriots, the Tea Act was a final indignity they could not tolerate.

In December of 1773, a group of patriots led by the charismatic Samuel Adams dressed up as Native Americans and snuck onto three ships anchored in Boston Harbor. The rebels dumped at least 340 chests of tea—more than 10,000 pounds—into the ocean. This event was the famous Boston Tea Party.

England promptly passed what became known as the Intolerable Acts. Some people also refer to these laws as the Coercive Acts. These included the Boston Port Act, the Administration of Justice Act, the Quartering Act, the Massachusetts Government Act, and the Quebec Act. Among other things, these laws resulted in the port of Boston being closed to all shipping except for food and fuels, and in British soldiers being permitted to occupy uninhabited buildings and, later, private homes if they so chose.

For the first time, the colonists realized that they had to

pull together instead of splitting into individual colonies. The First Continental Congress was held in September 1774. Representatives from twelve of the thirteen colonies attended.

Alarmed by this, England sent four more regiments of British troops to police the colonies. The patriots responded by forming their own militias and underground organizations. It was becoming increasingly clear that armed conflict was inevitable.

In April of 1775, British General Thomas Gage was ordered to send troops out of Concord to destroy a large supply of weapons. His other assignment was to capture two of the most powerful patriot leaders, Samuel Adams and John Hancock. So on the night of April 18th, General Gage sent a force of at least 700 men marching out to Concord.

Luckily, word of this raid leaked out, and a brave patriot named Paul Revere waited near the Charles River for the famous "one if by land, two if by sea" signal from his fellow rebels. When he saw the light flash in the tower of the Old North Church in Boston, he leaped onto his horse and began his famous ride to warn everyone.

Hearing the loud cries of "The British are coming!" John Hancock and Samuel Adams were able to escape long before the redcoats arrived. The British troops marched into the town of Lexington first. Approximately 50 militia members, called "minutemen," were waiting for them, holding muskets. There was a long, tense standoff, as neither side wanted to back down.

Then, suddenly, an unknown British soldier pulled the trigger. This was famously called "the shot heard 'round the world." Immediately, everyone else began firing. Once the flurry of shooting was over, the British troops continued their march into Concord. They found the arms depot and destroyed a number of weapons and shovels, as well as a supply of flour. Their mission accomplished, the redcoats began to march back to Boston.

More angry minutemen met them at the North Bridge in Concord, and there was another swift exchange of fire. The British were able to escape, but various groups of minutemen chased them all the way back to Boston. Almost 100 Americans were wounded or killed, while the British lost about 300 men.

Blood had been shed, and now there would be no turning back. The American Revolution had begun.

Three weeks later, the Second Continental Congress met in Philadelphia. This time, all thirteen colonies attended. They decided to form a Continental Army to replace the small militias, and a young but experienced soldier named George Washington was appointed to command it.

A few weeks after that, the first major battle of the Revolutionary War took place. It is called the Battle of Bunker Hill, but it actually took place on Breed's Hill. American troops initially occupied Bunker Hill, east of Boston, but then moved over to the strategically stronger Breed's Hill. Once there, they dug trenches and waited for the British to attack.

Under the command of Major General William Howe, the British did just that. England, expecting an easy victory, was surprised by the bravery and tenacity of the American soldiers. General Howe ordered his men not to fire until they could "see the whites of their eyes!" As a result, he lost almost 1,000 men in the battle, while the Americans had less than half that many casualties. The British ultimately managed to chase the patriots off the hill, but the battle cost them dearly. More than a third of the British forces had been killed or wounded.

In 1776, the colonies signed their Declaration of Independence and vowed to be a free and independent democratic country. The fighting went on for another seven bloody years, but in 1783, England finally conceded and signed a peace treaty.

The Thirteen Colonies were now the United States of America.

Beginning in 1620, when the Pilgrims landed at Plymouth Rock, the Thirteen Colonies were controlled by Britain. As the colonies became more established, the colonists grew tired of Britain's rules, and rebelled against taxes and trade laws by staging protests and boycotts. England responded by sending extra troops to occupy Massachusetts. The arrival of the troops in Boston Harbor on October 1, 1768, is depicted in this engraving by Paul Revere.

The British troops wore distinctive red uniforms and were known as redcoats. Some thought the uniforms resembled cooked lobsters — thus, the name lobsterbacks.

The Boston Massacre, one of the major clashes between the patriots and British soldiers, took place on March 5, 1770. After an angry mob of patriots threw snowballs at them, British troops responded with gunfire, as shown in Paul Revere's engraving. Several civilians were killed, including Crispus Attucks, considered by many to be the first person killed in the Revolutionary War.

After the British closed Boston Harbor to all shipping but food and fuel, and imposed more laws, the colonists decided to pull together. The First Continental Congress was held, and militias and underground organizations were formed. Taverns, traditionally places to do business or to gather with friends, were used often as meeting places for these underground organizations. The Lamb Tavern, top, is a typical tavern of the day. The interior may have looked something like this inn, bottom.

Tavern customers sometimes ordered a simple meal to go along with their beer or ale. The meat was cooked over an open flame using a turnspit, which allowed the meat to be cooked evenly. Larger dogs were trained to walk on the treadmill that turned the turnspit.

Printing presses like this one were used by the patriots to produce pamphlets and broadsides criticizing England for its tyranny and encouraging the people of the colonies to seek liberty.

This cartoon of a rattlesnake cut in segments represents the divided American colonies and was designed by Benjamin Franklin at the time of the Albany Congress of 1754. Franklin's rattlesnake appeared again in 1774 as a symbol of American unity against Britain.

A patriot who was convicted by the British of involvement in activities against England might be punished in any number of ways. The pillory, or stocks, held the hands and head up, forcing the imprisoned person to face the public.

Coded letters and encryption devices were sometimes used to communicate important information. These letters often used symbols or numbers in place of letters or words in case an important letter fell into enemy hands. This letter from General Henry Clinton, the British commander in New York, to General John Burgoyne uses an hourglass overlay to reveal a message.

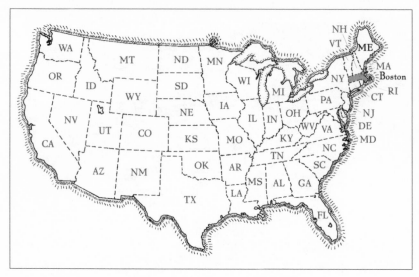

This modern map of the United States shows the location of Boston, Massachusetts.

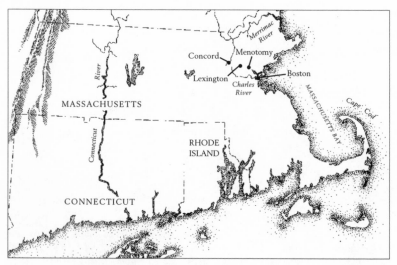

Lexington and Concord, in Massachusetts, were the sites of some of the earliest battles in the Revolutionary War.

About the Author

BARRY DENENBERG is the author of several critically acclaimed books for young readers, including two books in the Dear America series, *When Will This Cruel War Be Over?: The Civil War Diary of Emma Simpson*, which was named an NCSS Notable Children's Trade Book in the Field of Social Studies, and a YALSA Quick Pick; and *So Far From Home: The Diary of Mary Driscoll, an Irish Mill Girl*. Praised for his meticulous research, Barry Denenberg has written books about diverse times in American history, from the Civil War to Vietnam.

He says, "The American Revolution, more than any event in American history, has been presented to young readers as an abstract, artificial, distant, and disembodied occurrence involving old men who wore funny clothes and later became statues and oil paintings.

"After reading biographies of Thomas Jefferson and Sam Adams, and realizing how human and real they were, I set out to create William Thomas Emerson.

"I hoped to accomplish two things: to reveal, through the eyes of a young boy, what it was like to live in 1774 in Boston. And to bring the revolution to life by showing how it affected ordinary people and how they affected it."

Denenberg's nonfiction works include *An American Hero: The True Story of Charles A. Lindbergh*, which was named an ALA Best Book for Young Adults, and a New York Public Library Book for the Teen Age; and *Voices from Vietnam*, an ALA Best Book for Young Adults, a *Booklist* Editors' Choice, and a New York Public Library Book for the Teen Age. He lives with his wife and their daughter in Westchester County, New York.

This book is dedicated to
Phillip J. Gomez and Alicia N. Gomez

Acknowledgments

The author would like to thank Chris Kearin and his fellow "book people" for their help.

Grateful acknowledgment is made for permission to reprint the following:

Cover portrait: Sir Joshua Reynolds's *William Charles Colyear, Viscount Milsington (1747–1824), Later Third Earl of Portmore, As a Boy*, 1759.

Cover background: A detail from John Trumbull's *The Battle of Bunker's Hill*, 1786. The Granger Collection.

Interior illustrations copyright © 1998 by Heather Saunders.

Page 144 (top): Paul Revere's engraving of Boston Harbor,
     The American Revolution: A Picture Sourcebook,
     Dover Publications, Inc., New York.
Page 144 (bottom): British soldiers' uniforms, ibid.
Page 145: Paul Revere's engraving of the Boston Massacre, ibid.

Page 146 (top): The Lamb Tavern, Drake's *Old Boston Taverns*, W.A. Butterfield.

Page 146 (bottom): Interior of tavern, copyright © 1957 by Edwin Tunis. Copyright renewed © 1985 by Elizabeth H. Tunis. *Colonial Living*, published by HarperCollins Children's Publishers, 1976. Reprinted by permission of Curtis Brown, Ltd.

Page 147 (top): Turnspit dogs, ibid.

Page 147 (bottom): Colonial printing press, ibid.

Page 148 (top): Rattlesnake cartoon, *The American Revolution: A Picture Sourcebook*. Dover Publications, Inc., New York.

Page 148 (bottom): Pillory, reprinted with permission from *Curious Punishments of Bygone Days*, by Alice Morse Earle, by Applewood Books, Bedford, Massachusetts.

Page 149: Coded letter, Clements Library, University of Michigan.

Page 150: Maps by Heather Saunders.

Copyright © 1998 by Barry Denenberg
◆I◆

Library of Congress Cataloging-in-Publication Data
Denenberg, Barry.
The journal of William Thomas Emerson, a Revolutionary War patriot /
by Barry Denenberg. — 1st ed.
p.   cm. — (My name is America)
Summary: William, a twelve-year-old orphan, writes of his experiences in pre-Revolutionary War Boston where he joins the cause of the patriots who are opposed to British rule.
ISBN 0-590-31350-9 (paper over board)
1. Boston (Mass.)—History—Revolution, 1775–1783—Juvenile fiction.
2. United States—History—Revolution, 1775–1783—Juvenile fiction.   [1. Boston (Mass.)—History—Revolution, 1775–1783—Fiction. 2. United States—History—Revolution, 1775–1783—Fiction. 3. Orphans—Fiction. 4. Diaries—Fiction.]
I. Title. II. Series
PZ7.D4135Jo   1998
[Fic]—dc   97-52938
CIP   AC

ISBN 0-590-31350-9

10 9 8 7 6 5 4 3 2 1   8 9/9 0/0 01 02 03

The display type was set in Pelican.
The text type was set in Berling.
Book design by Pauline Neuwirth

Printed in the U.S.A.   37
First edition, September 1998
◆I◆

BOSTON HARBOR

A PLAN of
THE TOWN OF BOSTON
1775
MAP KEY

A. The Seven Stars Tavern
B. Armstrong's Book and Printing Shop
C. J. Williams- Instruments and Supplies
D. Fitch - Retail or Wholesale
E. Nelson's Bakery
F. Warehouse
G. Fanueil Hall
H. Dock Square
- - - One of William's Spy Routes

Scale of Yards

Cobb's Hill

Mill Pond

Valley Acre

Beacon Hill

Mount Whoredom

THE MALL

COMMON

Fox Hill

BATTLES STREET

Queen Street

Cornhill

Crooked Lane

Pudding Lane

King Street

Water Street

Mill Street

Newbury Street

Orange Street

Frog Lane

Mackerell Lane

Tanner's Lane

Cow Lane

Fort Hill

Rawe's Wharf

Griffin's Wharf

Long Wharf

Street

F   2-99 $10 −
DEN